I0542516

Secret Sensations

Sexy Stories Collection

VOLUME 10

10 EROTIC SHORT STORIES

SHALA BREECE

Publisher's Note: This is a work of fiction. Names,
characters, places, and incidents are a product of
the author's imagination. Locales and public
names are sometimes used for atmospheric
purposes. Any resemblance to actual people, living
or dead, or to businesses, companies, events,
institutions, or locales is completely coincidental.

Secret Sensations/ Shala Breece. -- 1st ed.
Xplicit Press, an imprint of TLM Media LLC

ISBN-13: 978-1-62327-541-9
ISBN-10: 1-62327-541-5
eISBN: 978-1-62327-591-4

Printed in the United States of America

CONTENTS

1 SECRETS OF AN EXOTIC DANCER

The music was blaring in the background, and the dressing room was busy as the partially naked females applied their make-up and donned their costumes. As Amy sat in front of her vanity, she could not help but admire her own beauty in the mirror. She often received compliments on her smooth, chocolate complexion and her thick, silky dark hair. Why was she even putting on this cheap make-up, when she was already the epitome of black perfection? An older looking blonde Caucasian woman walked up where she was seated.

"How do you do it, Amy? You never seem nervous. I've been doing this over ten years, and I still got butterflies in my stomach when I'm about to go out," the woman asked as she pulled a chair and sat next to Amy.

"I don't know Suz, it's just all bouts the

money with me, you know. I'll do whatever it took to got some paper," she replied and they both laughed at her bold confession.

It had been just over six years since Amy Johnson started working as an exotic dancer at one of Miami's most elite gentleman's club. Her best friend and mentor Suzie, or Suz, as she called her for short, had been employed there long before her. When she first started, out of all the girls there, Suzie was the only one who taught her how to maneuver and how to create a brand for herself with their clients.

Before working at this club, she had spent years waiting tables over at Denny's Bistro and could barely afford her rent and car note from her minimum wage salary. But now, with this new job, she was able to afford two cars - a convertible sports car and an SUV. She had also been able to move out of her crappy apartment in the projects, and now lived in a waterfront condo on the Miami Beach. Yes, life had improved a great deal for her with this job.

Therefore she was not ashamed or afraid to get on the stage, to do the job that paid for her high maintenance lifestyle.

"Ladies and gentlemen, Sherlock Boobs!" the announcer said on the microphone. Amy sprung from her seat; took a sip of water, put on her long black cloak and reading glasses, adjusted the blond wig she had on, and made her way from the dressing room to the stage. Sherlock Boobs had been her stage name for some time now, ever since she realized what a big hit it was, back in May when she first appeared in that costume. As she made her way to the pole, her eyes carefully scanned the audience of horny men.

There were some of her regular customers as well as some new faces. She grabbed hold of the pole and swerved her body in a seductive way around it, dropped down to the floor doing a complete split. The men went wild, they were cheering her on as their hungry eyes followed her every move. While still in her split position with her legs parted in different directions, she bent her head downwards, and popped open her cloak. "Take it out, take it out!" several of the men shouted, as she stood up seductively grinding her body against the pole. Her breasts were bare under the cloak and she had only a black lace thong on. She made small circles around the pole and then slowly dropped the cloak to the floor, exposing her huge, gorgeous, melon shaped breasts to the men. Considering the fact that she was seasoned and experienced, she could never understand why she would become so aroused when she danced on stage. Probably it was because of her own emotional attachment with her job that she had been able to project such a seductive character.

As she worked her way around the pole, her huge breasts bounced a little from the movements. Suddenly there was an explosion of water on the stage, and she was showered right there on the stage in her black thong and knee high boots. She could hear the sounds of the pleased men in the audience. She continued to move her body seductively around the pole, turning around, and bending over one time, to give her audience a look at her perfectly shaped ass. Soon she made her way off the stage and into the audience to give lap dances to the highest paying customers.

There was a handsome dark-eyed gentlemen seated in the back. He wore a navy blue suit and he seemed like he could afford her. She swiftly made her way to him, and hopped over his legs. He slipped a hundred dollar bill into the sides of her thong. Her heart pounded as his hot, masculine hands slowly glided along her body. Normally she did not approve of the customer physically touching her, unless it was a private session, but there was something about this handsome stranger that had her wanting to feel his touch, his lips, his everything.

His eyes examined every inch of her body. He kept licking his lips and the way his leg shook nervously, she could tell that this was probably his first time at the club, and possibly even his first professional lap dance. She looked into his desire filled eyes, and pressed her pussy down hard against his crotch. She ground her wet pussy up against his groin area, the thin layer of lace was not enough. He moved his hands over her naked breasts and fondled them with soft gentle massages. She almost screamed out in pleasure.

Who was this man, and why was she so susceptible to his touch. She could hear him panting as she increased the momentum of her grinds. She stood up and turned around with her back facing him, she giggled her ass in front of him. He was impressed because he took that opportunity and gave her two hard smacks across her ass. She looked back and smiled at him.

They were two grown people and they knew exactly what was going on. She was seducing him with her lap dance, and now the urge to fuck her was even greater than before. He grabbed her tiny waist, and sat her down on his groin area again. She continued her slow movements against his pants. Soon she felt his hard erection almost piercing through his pants, she looked at him smiling.

"I do offer private sessions, in the back," she whispered in his ear, as she nibbled them a little. Again he pulled out his wallet, and slipped three hundred dollars this time, into her hand. "I'll see you in the back then," he whispered with a wicked look in his eyes.

"My turn, my turn," another man who was behind her shouted, she had been so enjoying the chemistry between them, that she had forgotten about her other clients.

"Give me ten minutes," she whispered to him. "I'll send someone to get you when I'm done," she whispered his ear, as she got up and went to service her next client.

This man was nothing like the previous client, he gave her about three twenty dollar notes, which was like petty cash for her. He was an older African American guy, with a bald head. He was wearing a simple polo shirt with khaki pants, and he kept his hands to himself as he enjoyed her erotic motions on his lap.

Unlike the previous man, she could tell this was not his first time receiving a lap dance. Soon he planted another couple of twenties in her panties and after a while of grinding on his groin, she got off him, and went over to the next highest bidder, using the same techniques she had used on the first two men. She made another couple of hundreds from this other client.

"It was a good night," she sighed as she made her way to the dressing room. Thoughts of the first client kept lingering in her mind and soon she found herself sneaking through the crowd of men trying to find him.

"Hey. You're back," a voice said from behind her, as she felt him grab her hand. She turned around and her heart flipped when her eyes met his. He had moved around the room a little, and he now stood in an area with a little more light. She could now carefully examine his body as the light gleamed upon his skin. He looked like an athlete. He was lean and tall, with a skin tone close to hers and he had wavy black hair. As she drew nearer to him, her heart pounded and she felt the strong currents of desire pulling the together. She led him back to her dressing room; most of the other girls had either gone home or were now working on the stage, and in the crowd. She locked the door behind them, and proceeded to dim the lights in the room. He looked on with curious eyes as if trying to anticipate her next move. She instructed him to sit in a black leather chair, while she stood in front of him, moving her body seductively to the music that played in the background. He was licking his lips again, and she could see the flames of desire in his ears. She glided her hands all over her body, as she stared him directly in the eye.

She finally removed the blonde wig, revealing her beautiful black hair that was hidden underneath. He leaned back in the chair as he enjoyed the private show that she was putting on for him. Yes, she was horny, and wanted to fuck him, her pussy was wet and her nipples were hard. She slowly caressed her nipples with her index finger and her thumb.

Then, she did something that he did not at all expect. She brought her lips downwards as she held one breast up to her mouth, she stretched her tongue out and when her tongue made contact with her nipple, his eyes nearly popped out. He opened his legs wider and unzipped his pants, pulling out his long erect penis. Amy almost stopped what she was doing when she saw the full length of his dick. This was by far the longest, biggest dick she had ever seen. It was slightly bent at the top, and the thickness and width of the dick itself was like no other. He could tell that she was impressed because he smiled in the corner of his lips as he watched her.

She would have continued the lap dance that she had started but she just could not resist the urge to get down on her knees and suck his big dick. And so, she followed her heart and did just that. Her warm lips on his cock sent shock waves through his body, and she carefully worked her way upwards and downwards on it with her tongue. While she had one hand at the base of his dick, her other hand was busy between her legs, rubbing on her clit. Her pussy was dripping wet, and the more she sucked his cock, the more she wanted him to fuck her. She used her tongue and flicked it over the head of his dick a couple of times and it stiffened even more. Then using her tongue like a wash cloth, she made sure she licked every inch of his huge tool.

He gripped the arm rest of the chair, as the sensations he felt on his dick took control of his every movement. He groaned out loud, asking her not to stop, calling her a bad bitch and then even one time saying he felt like he was in heaven. Every time she heard him groan out loud, she too experienced her arousal getting stronger.

Finally she stood up to her feet, and sat on his erect dick with her wet pussy, gliding down its full length. He gripped her tightly onto it and shoved it inside of her good and hard. She moaned out when she felt the entire dick in her pussy. She began making slow steady movements up and down his dick with her pussy, stopping when she got to the base, and grinding her pussy a little. She moaned out loud when she felt the grip of his mouth on her nipples and her movements intensified in accordance with the way he increased the suction that he had on her hard nipples.

"Oh yeah, fuck me," he groaned as she rode his dick relentlessly with her pussy. She could feel her insides ripping apart, and she knew that his monstrous cock was definitely doing some damage in there. As she continued popping her pussy up and down on his dick, his dick began acting out on its own, ramming inside her violently.

Suddenly it was like he lost all control, and as she looked into his eyes she saw that he was totally consumed with passion, he drove his dick upwards inside her pussy so hard that she was crying for him to stop. "No, I ain't gonna stop, you're gonna took this dick today," he said as he grabbed hold of her tiny waist and continued to bang her pussy, endlessly. Thrust after thrust was harder and rougher than the one before, and the pain of the thrust soon turned into a sick, twisted type of sweet pleasure. Amy now found herself moving her pussy to meet his dick half way, as her huge breasts bounced back and forth in his mouth. They fucked and fucked, and their moans were loud and full of passion.

"Oh God, I'm gonna cum," he groaned as he gave her a hard thrust that almost caused her pussy to crack open. He exploded his hot semen inside her wet pussy, the sensations that she felt from this hot cum showering the inner walls of her pussy caused her to reach her climax. With a loud moan, of "Oh Yesssssss," she, too, exploded and her juices met his and they savored their ecstasy together,

The call had come suddenly in the middle of the day while she was at home watching TV. It seemed like just last week she and her best friend Suzie were together having fun, now the news of her being terribly ill at the hospital was like a hard pill to swallow. She quickly got dressed and made her way to the hospital to support her friend. When she got there, Suzie did not look well. As she spoke to her, Amy realized that her friend had been concealing the fact that she was feeling ill and growing weaker and weaker by the day.

"Did the doctor tell you exactly what wrong Suz?" she asked with a look of concern on her face. Suzie had been like a mother to her; she had taken her under her wings, and showed her everything there was to know about the business. Amy remembered the time when she just started working at the club and she was about to get evicted from her apartment - it had only been about a week since she had met Suzie.

Yet upon hearing the news, Suzie had offered her rent money to pay for the next two months so she could keep her apartment, and this was not the only time Suzie had gotten her out of a bad situation.

Amy almost fell off the bed in shock when she heard the answer to her question. "What!" she shrieked. "How? No! This can't be true. Tell them you want another test. Tests can be wrong sometimes," she continued as she refused to accept the information conveyed to her.

For Amy this was like a nightmare. She had lost her mom as a child, and then her dad a few years ago, and now she was about to lose her best friend.

"Listen to me Amy, I have accepted it. I made some poor decisions, and now this was the consequences of my actions." Suzie pleaded with her. "You need to leave the club, find another type of job; it's not worth losing your life. AIDS was not written across anybody's forehead," she continued as tears were now running down her cheeks. Out of hundreds and thousands of strippers and exotic dancers around the world, why did her best friend had to be the one to got AIDS? They all did it from time to time... a client would walk in and if he could pay, they would give him a private session and yes, sex was included.

In fact she had given a private session to an attractive mysterious man. Could he too be spreading the disease? The thought of how she could very well have AIDS, made her sick to her stomach. As soon as the doctor walked into the room, she asked him about information on how she could get tested for the disease.

Amy was so relieved when she received the results of her HIV test. Negative, great! She thought to herself as she breathed a sigh of relief. It had been about three weeks since she had received the news that her best friend Suzie had AIDS in the advanced stages. Amy was now suspicious of every client she met and she was definitely not having unprotected sex with any random guy. What had happened to Suzie had scared her to the point to where she was actually thinking about quitting her job at the club. Was it really worth it? She knew that she did not want to lose her life to AIDS just for some extra money. However, she did not know what she would do if she were to quit. She was not college educated, and most probably she would have to go back to working endless hours for minimum wage.

As Amy made her way onto the stage, she scanned the audience of men as she would usually do. However tonight something was different. Her heart almost skipped a beat when she locked gazes with the mysterious man that she had met once before in the past. She watched him as she worked the stage, gliding her body down and around the stripper pole. Tonight she had been wearing a firefighter costume. As she stripped the costume off, the crowd of men roared with cheers of satisfaction. She moved her body seductively to the rhythm of the music while she sneaked little glances at the stranger. The entire time she was on the stage - for the first time ever - she felt butterflies in her stomach and she could not shake the nervous feeling.

Amy went about doing her usual dance routine on the pole, but tonight she did not give any lap dances tonight. When she got done she made her way back to the dressing room. As she got closer to the door, she could see the figure of a man standing at the entrance. It was the guy who had captured her attention during the show. Feeling nervous she tried to sneak inside without even looking at him.

She felt his strong hand grip her arm as she tried to escape from him. "Don't act like you didn't see me. Why don't we get to know each other?" he said as he held onto her arm awaiting a response.

She did not know why he wanted to get to know her; after all, if he was looking for sex, they had done it already. "Why were you so interested in getting to know me?" she asked him with a suspicious look on her face. Was he married, was he a cop trying got a case on her or even worse, was he a guy sleeping around spreading diseases? Although she was hot for him, there were so many unanswered questions that she had on her mind.

"Firstly, could I have your name?" he asked, extending his hand out for a handshake. "I'm Amy, and you?" she replied, still looking at him suspiciously.

"I'm Tony," he replied with a smile on his face. He told her that he was interested in her, because he was very attracted to her; she was a beautiful black woman whom he wanted to spend time getting to know.

Amy went outside to the parking lot with him, and they sat on the hood of his car as they got to know each other better. Although he had originally said he would not disclose his profession to her, as the night went on, they got more and more comfortable around each other.

He was an established therapist with a private office in the city. He had decided to come to the gentleman's club after one of his friends recommended that he go out and had some fun. Over a year ago he had lost his wife and daughter in a terrible car crash. When she heard about the tragic demise of his wife and child her heart felt for him, and she wanted to embrace him and took away his pain. As they spoke she could feel her nipples hardening and peeking through her blouse. His eyes caught a glimpse of her pierced nipples and he instantly leaned in and planted a kiss on her soft lips. Tony spread her legs and stroked the insides of her wet pussy with index finger, she moaned with pleasure, and begged him not to stop.

As she lay there on her back, she unbuttoned her blouse and her huge set of breasts were exposed. He licked the hard nipples; caressed each one slowly while his fingers explored her pussy. Suddenly a light flashed from a car driving by and they were reminded that they were in the parking lot of a public place. No, he did not want to do her like that; he pulled away, and said, "Not like this, not here, let's go to my place." He opened the door for her to get in his car. As she got in the car, her pussy ached for his dick and the ten minute ride to his house seemed like hours. They barely made it through the front door when their lips locked in a long, passionate, hard kiss. As they kissed they were moving around the cramped living room, knocking stuff off the shelves as they let their feelings got the best of them. Finally they made it to the bed. He had her exactly where he to be from the first time he had seen her.

And now that she was there in his bed, he was going to devour her pussy with tongue and dick. He spread her legs open, as he put his face between them.

Amy moaned loud, when she felt his hot tongue flicking back and forth on her wet pussy. Tony held onto her legs as if trying to keep her steady. The sensations running through her body were magical. Tony knew exactly what to do, to increase the pleasure of this woman. He used his tongue to penetrate through the inside flesh of her wet pussy.

"Oh God, yeah!" she moaned out as he wiggled his tongue back and forth, inside her pussy. He then focused his attention on her clit. He stroked it gently with his tongue at first, but when that was not enough he began sucking on it. Her clitoris was swollen with desire and she could not remain still as this cunnilingus master fulfilled her desires. She found herself moaning and saying stuff that not even she could understand. Her eyes were rolling to the back of her head.

"Fuck me, baby please, I need your dick inside my pussy," she moaned with a voice full of yearning.

When he heard that, Tony did not make her ask him a second time. He released the grip that he had on her clit and proceeded to tease her a little with his dick. He rubbed his dick back and forth around the opening of her vagina, teasing her. As he prepared to fuck her, he kept a steady gaze into her longing eyes. Like a monster had taken over her, she grabbed hold of his dick, and tried to force him to thrust it between the crack of her pussy. He looked surprised, but welcomed her sudden bold move. In fact, he was turned on even more. His dick was throbbing the entire time, and he felt a little relief as it made its way down into her hot, wet cunt. He could feel her pussy expanding to accommodate his huge dick, and kissed her softly as he continued the journey inside of her.

"Yeah, baby, don't stop. Oh yeah," she moaned as he began to thrust his dick in and out of her pussy. Each thrust was sweeter and harder than the one before. He pulled the dick out and rubbed the head of it on her swollen clit and she moaned when she felt his new move. He then, without warning slammed the dick back inside her with much more force. She felt his dick ripping the insides of her pussy. He continued fucking her, giving her long hard thrust with his wickedly huge dick, and then increasing his momentum. She closed her eyes as she enjoyed the feeling of being fucked by a monster cock. She loved it. Her tiny pussy was stretched, used and abused, when she couldn't take it anymore, she cried out for her momma. It was the most amazing sex that she ever had, she felt like she was in a sweet place, where her juices were flowing freely out of her pussy.

His thrusts increased to an even greater degree when she looked up into his eyes as he was riding her pussy. She saw his eyes completely engulfed with the flames of desire. He gripped her waist and continued to give her quick hard thrusts. "Oh shit, this is the best pussy ever," he groaned as she felt him approaching his brink. She too, was almost at the summit of her ecstasy. Their bodies moved in corresponding movements and with several hard quick thrusts, they both exploded together. He rolled over to the side of her as he tried to calm down from his ecstasy. As they lay in the bed they spent the entire evening talking further, and getting to know each other some more.

The following morning Amy woke up in the arms of her new friend and lover. She looked over at him and he was such a cute, handsome man. She did not want to got out of the bed. It seemed like she was dreaming and she did not want it to end.

Her phone rang, and she swiftly made her way out of the bed to answer it. It was Suzie's doctor on the phone; he asked her if she knew of any living relatives that Suzie might have. Hearing that from the doctor was not a good sign and she begged him to tell her what was going on. Tony had awoken to the sound of the phone ringing; he sat in the bed with a confused gaze. "What's wrong?" he asked her.

She did not even have time to really explain all what that had been going on to him. All she told him was that her friend was in the hospital and that was her doctor on the phone. Since she did not had her car with her, he got up and put a shirt on. He sped through the early morning traffic to get her to the hospital.

Amy dropped down to her knees and cried out; in such sorrow that it broke his heart. She had just found out that her best friend died and she was not ready to accept the bad news. "How, why, noooooooooooo!" she cried as she sat on the hospital floor. Tony came to her and picked her up, supporting her as the doctor proceeded to pass on some further information to her.

Suzie had no registered family. She had been an orphan, and had no children. Amy was the closest thing she had to family. As the doctor continued his interview with her, he mentioned that she had handed him her will before she died, and had asked him to give it to Amy, her best friend.

Amy followed the doctor to his office where he privately handed her the folded document. Sure enough it was her will. She had left Amy the sum of $200,000: her life's savings, along with her house and car.

Her only requests were that Amy stop stripping and use the money to set up a business. "She left me her life's savings," Amy said as she wept right there in the doctor's office. Even in her death, Suzie had cared about her so much that she left her money to start up her own business. Tony came around to where she was standing and hugged her tightly, whispering to her "I'm here with you know, God knows why we met."

She laid her head on his warm, comforting chest and replied, "She was really an angel on earth." As she spoke fresh streams of tears made their way down her cheeks.

Amy never went back to the strip club after

that. She set up a small restaurant, and this time she was not the one waiting tables. Her husband, Tony, co-owned the restaurant with her, and he too had put his strip club days behind him.

As she lay on the small bed, she looked at the doctor eagerly; as he looked at the screen in front him. "Congratulations, Mr. and Mrs. Anderson, it looks like there's definitely a little baby in there. From what I cn see, it looks like a girl, but it might be too early to tell for sure."

Tony's smile brightened up the entire room, and both their hearts flipped with joy when they received the confirmation of her pregnancy from the doctor. Considering all the things that she had been through, Amy vowed to raise her daughter right; she would never let her child know about her exotic dancing days. It would remain a secret between her and her husband.

2 RING OF THORNS

Lilly rushed out of the house in a frantic effort to get to her car. Her jet black curls flowed with the wind and softly brushed her high cheekbones and dimpled cheeks. They had run out of food at the house and her stomach was growling with hunger. The grocery store was about five minutes away from her husband's office. Lilly and Perry Jenkins had been married for over ten years, with two beautiful girls.

That morning they had a horrible argument about her paranoia over him spending long hours at the office. She was extremely insecure about her husband, and when she found some suspicious text messages on his phone, her paranoia kicked into high gear. As the morning progressed, she had time to think and reflect on everything she said, and she had to admit that she probably overreacted a little over the text messages.

Why would he cheat? He was a happily married man who loved his wife more than anything else in the world. No other woman would compare to her! She had loved this man with her everything and he would be a fool to throw their marriage down the drain over some little fling. So what if her husband was a tall, black, muscular man with brown eyes and pink lips? She was equally as beautiful with a smooth, caramel skin tone, light gray eyes, and a million dollar smile.

They were a beautiful couple. She did not know what she could possibly be worried about. These thoughts engulfed her as she pulled into the all too familiar grocery store. She got out and breathed in the fresh Mississippi air of grass and cigarettes. As she walked between the aisles in the store, she picked up some basic food items for them and grabbed a sandwich on her way out at the small counter. Since it was almost lunch time, she would go over to Perry's office to drop off the sandwich for him.

Perry worked as an art check and shared a small office with his business partner, Thomas Gage. A third person also worked at this office, much to her disgust. Jennifer Stewart worked as the secretary for the two men, and she was every wife's nightmare. She was a young, attractive, witty, blonde woman.

"What the hell!" She gasped when she saw the scene that greeted her behind the door of her husband's office. Jen was running her fingers through her silk blonde hair, as her naked body bounced up and down on Perry's dick. The sound of his wife's voice caused

Perry to immediately push his mistress off him, and he sprung up from his chair, with his erect dick hanging out as he tried to apologize to his angry wife.

"How could you, do this?" she asked, as a look of anger and disbelief took over the heavenly innocence. He hurriedly tried to zip his pants and fasten the buttons of his shirt, while his secretary had literally run out of the office at the site of seeing his angry wife.

He was moving in closer to her, apologizing profusely, saying he did not know what had taken over him, and this was the first and the last time, he would never do anything like that.

His pleas fell on deaf ears as the hurt and anger kept intensifying through Lilly's body. A dangerous feeling of pure hate came over her, and without even thinking twice, she went into a violent spur. Her words were harsh and her blows were swift and very manly; she did not care, she just wanted to hurt him back, and it did not matter how she went about doing it. He kept trying to grab hold of her hand, to put an end to her hitting him. Finally, she stopped her attack and looked directly into his eyes. "I hate you, I wish you would die, like the cheating dog that you are!"

With that, she left his office, banging every door on her way out. He had never seen her so upset before, and it broke his heart, the way she coldly dismissed him. Perry vowed to himself that he would get his wife back.

It had been three weeks since she caught her husband cheating with his secretary, and every day since that unforgettable day, he would get down on his knees begging her to forgive him. They lived in the same house but slept in different beds.

Their wedding anniversary was around the corner, and she had absolutely nothing to celebrate about. Considering what had happened, she was definitely not going to do anything special on that day. Had it not been for her two children, she would have served him with divorce papers. The image of Jennifer, riding her husband's dick, kept replaying in her mind, and she just could not stomach being around him too much.

The morning of their anniversary, she got up and went about her morning with indifference. She went downstairs to the kitchen, but Perry was not there apologizing to her, like he would normally do since the incident. However, she did see a note that he left her. It read:

"I would never give up on us, Happy Anniversary, my love. I know we had had problems recently, but my feelings for you had never changed. I am truly sorry from the bottom of my heart. I love you.

"P.S Please have dinner with me tonight at The Jet."

Although in her heart she was beginning to forgive him, she was trying hard to keep on hating him. After all, what type of woman walks in on her husband with secretary having sex, and forgives him. Only a FOOL.

Throughout the day, Lilly could not shake off her desire to meet her husband for dinner. She wanted to hear him apologize once more. She also had lots of unanswered questions that she needed to ask him. When the afternoon time came, she decided that she would accept his dinner proposal. She picked up her cell and dialled his number; he picked up by the second ring. He was so happy to hear that she had decided to join him for dinner.

She wore a mid-length black lace dress, with a deep V-cut in the front that exposed her delicious looking cleavage. When he saw her at the restaurant, his eyes nearly popped out with desire, and she could see that he was nervous and uneasy around her.

He, too, looked mighty fine in his black tux. Her heart raced when she saw him, and she hated herself for allowing herself to fall into his trap. As they had dinner, they reminisced about their past, and she suddenly felt a little better about him. She did not even ask him any of the questions that she had rehearsed in her mind. After dinner, they dropped the top down in his convertible and drove around the neighborhood; they were fondling each other like they did when they were young lovers.

Perry had arranged for the girls to stay with his parents for the night, and so they had the house to themselves when they got home. As they made their way upstairs, although they had a great time, Lilly could not forget what she had seen. All was not well with them. As she opened the door to the master bedroom, her jaw dropped open and she was speechless. Their room was adorned with red rose petals everywhere. She turned back and he was standing right behind her waiting. Their lips met, and it seemed like it was their first time. Their kiss was wet and full of passion and Lilly could feel his erect dick grinding against their fabric. "God I've missed you," he groaned as he ran his finger down the feminine curves of her body.

Perry swept her up and cradled her in his strong, masculine arms as he carried her over to the romantically decorated bed. Her body looked amazing as she now became the centerpiece of the bed covered in red rose petals. He kissed her on her soft, tender lips that were warm and he transferred tiny waves of desire to her body that peaked her arousal. She moaned out as she felt herself getting lost in his tender caress.

Perry gently parted her long, clean shaved legs and slowly indulged on her delicate skin with his tongue. She whimpered at the feel of his hot, wet tongue all over her body. He worked his way upwards, between her legs. She moaned in sheer ecstasy when his tongue reached its destination. He slowly flicked his tongue on her swollen clit, and then gave it a hard suck. He now had her, wet and vulnerable; he licked and sucked every inch of her wet pussy. Her juices were oozing out of her pussy, and her fingers were digging into the linen of the sheets. His tongue lingered inside her pussy, as he now had the fingers of his outstretched arm caress her nipples. She wanted more and begged for him to suck her pussy some more. She found herself, using her hand on his head, forcing it to remain locked down between her legs. He lavished her pussy with his tongue as he ran it up and down, in and out of her moist heat.

As he sucked her pussy, his dick throbbed with desire, wishing that would trade places with his tongue. He could not resist anymore; he pulled his tongue out of her pussy and stroked his hard dick a few times. Without warning, she plunged its full length inside her pussy, which caused a loud gasp to escape her full lips. He continued to thrust it inside, while holding onto the back of her head while his tongue kept her tongue engaged in a series of hot wet kissed. "Oh God, baby," he groaned as he pulled out his full length and shoved it back in with great force. As they fucked, the bed rocked and the sound of the springs could be heard, along with her loud thrills of pleasure.

He gave her long hard strokes and then increased his momentum to shorter, quicker thrusts. She was holding onto his arms as her body rocked back and forth as it received the harsh pounding. He managed to slip in, "I'm sorry baby," as he penetrated her.

As far as she was concerned, at the moment, all was very well. Her pussy was like her brain right now; she was very pleased and so whatever had happened was well forgiven. He continued to penetrate her insides while now caressing her hard nipples with his hot tongue. She moaned and moaned, under the intense pressure of these magical sensations. "Oh yeah, Perry, don't stop," she shrieked as he gave pulled on her nipples as his dick explored her insides. The more they fucked the more she wanted to feel more of him inside her. Deeper and deeper he went, until he could almost feel her uterus.

She could feel her juices making their way down her spine, and tiny spasms caused her flesh to viciously lock onto his dick. He was now also at the brink of his explosion and he was trying hard not to release. He stroked her insides over and over again, with his tool, and the more he tried to resist his ejaculation, the wilder his thrusts became. Finally, he let a loud groan, as he jerked his dick one last time inside her. His hot juices exploded inside her moist opening; she too had also reached her climax and their bodies rocked together trying to find its way back to reality.

That night they slept in each other's embraces, and it seemed like all was forgiven, and they were both happy.

Over the next few weeks, after Perry had apologized profusely, and even proved his point by spending less time at the office and more time at home with the family. She had not forgotten his lapse in judgment, but she had forgiven him. She laid in the lounge on the back porch as she thought about her booked schedule for the weekend. They had planned to go to Disney World to give their family the bond that it once possessed and had lost over the years. Their daughters—Daisy, age 7, and Steffi, age 4—were miracles, and she loved them unconditionally. She felt that they did not deserve to be neglected by their dad, and that was why she planned the trip.

They looked over at the astronomical sign pointing to the Splash Mountain, a roller coaster at Disney World. Daisy rushed off into the distance to gaze in awe at the large Mickey Mouse costume holding balloons.

The whole family seemed to be enjoying the trip, and Lilly was even glad that she had come. The last night there was like a dream, as they laid pillows on the floor of the spacious hotel room; Lilly glanced at her husband and caught him staring at her with such a loving look in his eyes that it almost took her breath away. Daisy and Steffi sat at the fireplace roasting marshmallows and making s'mores, while Perry laid back, glancing at them from time to time.

"I'm glad we came here," Lilly said dreamily. She gazed longingly into the fire as if she was in a trance. He smiled at her and came closer, taking her hand in his.

"I'm glad we did too; they seemed to have had fun," He gestured toward the cute girls sitting and chatting animatedly by the fire. She truly felt as if they had grown closer within the weekend, but tomorrow was Monday, and there was a busy week ahead of her.

The family arrived back in Mississippi at 7

AM the next morning, and Lilly had to rush to work without even stopping for breakfast. She had plenty to do before the conference tomorrow and she had to start as soon as possible. She sat at her desk in her corner office and made the appointment with Dave Javier, a guest speaker for her employee appreciation conference.

He was at a hotel two miles away, and she had to go pick him up tomorrow at precisely 9 AM. Everything was still going smoothly as she pulled into her driveway that night, and her husband greeted her at the door with a bear hug and a passionate kiss. She could see that something was wrong, even with the kiss, because he seemed distant. She noticed even with the short bits of subtle remarks that he was not as peppy as he had been that last weekend.

"What's wrong?" She asked and he threw her a look that said that he did not want to talk. He probably had a horrible day at the office and just didn't want to talk about it. All the bells in her head were ringing in her to just let it go, but stubbornly, she persisted. "Did you have a bad day at the office?" She questioned and he continued eating his dinner as if she had not spoken.

"Nothing," he replied, short and expressionless. She put her head down and focused on the plate filled with lasagne and chicken wings. Daisy and Steffi both finished up their plates and asked to be excused. Lilly nodded and got up. She did not want to be at that table while her husband was so upset. He did not even want to talk to her about it. She climbed the stairs to the master bedroom and lay on the bed. She cried herself to sleep.

When she got up the next morning, the bed was empty. She looked over and saw that Perry's side was still made up; he hadn't even slept there. She rustled out of bed and lumbered down the stairs. She slept in, so everyone was gone. When she looked at the time, it was 8:05 AM. She showered and put on a red pants suit. She always felt comfortable in red. She left the house and got into her Chevrolet.

Arriving at the Mark Adams hotel, Lilly looked suspiciously at the red Mercedes. What's he doing here? She wondered, as she examined the vehicle more carefully. She continued fretting as she walked to the reception.

"Hi, my husband said he would be here today and my youngest daughter just got admitted into the hospital. I really need to see him to let him know. His name was Perry Banks, was there any way...." She had barely finished speaking when the receptionist, who sat in a brown suit with wire rimmed glasses, interrupted her.

"Sorry, but it's against company policy to..." She glanced at Lilly and saw her pleading eyes.

"Please, you as a woman would understand the responsibility that a mother would hold for her family when one member was sick. So I would expect you of all people to know that when I need to see my husband, I need to see him now." She appealed to her. The receptionist looked pensive for a moment. Then she spoke up.

"He's in room 403B," she said and gave her a slim gold card. "Use it wisely."

She then scurried back to her work and paid no attention, as Lilly calmly walked to the elevator. He was not supposed to be at hotels. He was an architect. Wasn't he supposed to be working on sketches in the office, or at a construction site? What was he doing here? The question pressed at her until she reached the fourth floor. She searched the room plates until she found 403B. She pushed the card into the door, and it clicked open. She stared, heartbroken, at Jennifer and Perry both naked at the wet bar in the corner of the room. Her hands lay on his thigh and they sprang up to her mouth when she saw Lilly staring at them. Lilly could not speak.

"Oh my God, I am so sorry Lilly, honey," Perry apologized, but Lilly remained motionless.

"Again? I can't believe you did this to me again! I thought you had changed!!!" She shrieked and then pointed her anger to Jennifer as she spoke up.

"I'm sorry about this Mrs. Banks, but Mr. Banks and I did not intend to hurt you like this. It just happened." Jennifer rushed to the sofa and threw on a maroon bath robe.

"You bitch! You didn't intend?" Lilly walked up to her and slapped her across her face. She was getting tired of the same routine over and over again. She was getting tired of Perry's infidelity. She sped down the street, the conference forgotten. As she arrived in the serene neighborhood, it dawned on her as to what she should do. She took out her phone and dialled.

"Two times, you've caught him cheating? What did you do the second time?" Amanda, her best friend asked, as they sipped iced tea on the patio next to her pool.

"I slapped Jennifer, and I threw Perry out. As far as I know, that's just about sufficient." She answered and looked over the pool at the cat lazily stretching on the lawn.

"Well, I would help," Amanda spoke quietly, "Here was the number of Carl Bafer, my divorce attorney when I was going through my thing with Chris," she said talking about her ex-husband. She had been divorced for over five years and happier now more than ever.

"Thanks, I'll go see him tomorrow," she smiled. She knew that Perry was going to get exactly what he deserved.

The next morning, at exactly 10 AM, she knocked on the red door of Mr. Carl Bafer, and he opened it almost immediately. He was wearing a slick black suit and a red tie. He was a sturdy black man, and he looked like an important lawyer. She felt at peace when she walked into the leather pleated office.

"Hi," he smiled at her and she smiled back. "Why don't you tell me about yourself and your marriage," he said, and she could not stop smiling at him.

She could tell that she was attracted to

him, but did not know how to express it. He was slightly younger than she had imagined he would have been. His gray eyes locked with hers as she explained her frustration with her husband's infidelity to this handsome stranger. He provided her with some court documents to sign as they began what would be the first in a three step divorce process.

As the weeks went by, Lilly's visit and calls to Carl Bafer became more frequent. The more they spent time with each other, the more the attraction that she felt for him increased. It had now gotten to the point where she was always trying to find some excuse to go over to his office, and he too was mutually attracted to her. When she did not call him, he would call her. Sometimes just to find out how her day had been going. The two of them finally decided to step up and admit the attraction between them. They set up a dinner date at one of the most exquisite restaurants in the town.

As she made her way to the black convertible parked outside her door, she could not help but notice his cool calm composure as he tilted his head back in the front seat with an upward stare of the evening sky. He had his top dropped down and he looked like a modern version of her new prince charming. She wore a sexy black and white lace tube dress, with red stilettos, and her hair was seductively pinned upwards. "Wow, you look amazing," he said, as he made his way around the car to open her door. She got in the car, equally impressed by his black turtleneck and silk black pants. They drove off into the night as they chatted about everything, from her divorce to the Mississippi weather.

They had a lovely dinner and things really started heating up when they got to her front door after a well-spent evening. Her kids were with her parents for the weekend, and she was alone in her huge home. He must have sensed her loneliness because he offered to keep her company for the rest of the night. At first she was a bit hesitant, but desires got the best of her and she found herself now longing to share at least a kiss with him. They sat on the couch next to each other, and she popped in the DVD of one of her favorite movies, "Pretty Woman."

They drew in closer to each other as the movie begun and soon she felt his gentle caress on her legs. She looked up at him, with a look of consent in her eyes as he proceeded to further explore her body with his fingers. He finally leaned in even closer, and when their lips met, he planted a soft kiss on them. Instantly, flames of desire were ignited, and she grabbed onto his lips with her desire-filled ones. Their kisses were hot, wet, and full of passion. They moaned as their tongues wrestled together in a tug of passion. He now had her under him and was slowly undressing her, while she had been distracted by his kissed.

His lips left her, and his tongue slowly

made its way down to her two full peaks. From the look of her round, hard, nipples, he could tell that she was already aroused. It had been a while since she felt the tender touch of a man all over her body and she whimpered under his touch, begging him for more. Her moans were in a stretched tone as she tried hard to control herself. He noticed what she was doing, and although he was enjoying the moment, he wanted all of her. He knew exactly what to do to get her to give it all to him. He quickly left her nipples and glided his tongue downwards past her navel and to her wet pussy. When she felt his tongue on her clitoris, she pulled back a little from the intensity of his tongue on her. He quickly pulled her back onto his waiting tongue, and plunged it in her moist center as he devoured her raw.

Tiny spasms jolt down her body as her juices run down her spices and brought her to sweet surrender. She was enjoying everything about Mr. Carl Bafer. The way he handled her divorce, the way he was handling her pussy, everything.

Carl could tell that she was enjoying herself. He had a knack for trying to read people's minds. He continued pleasuring her with his wicked tongue, as his index finger made its way into her pussy to assist his tongue. She moaned out loud at the feel of his finger inside her. He used his finger and gently massaged her clitoris, while his tongue flicked back and forth further downwards around the small opening of the pussy. "Oh yeah, Carl... Carl... Yeah... Oh yeah," she found herself moaning as she ground her pussy against his entire face. She could feel that she was about to reach the peak of her climax, and she almost did when he released his hold on her pussy.

He felt her body tensing up. The tiny contractions of her pussy had become quicker and he knew that she was probably about to climax. He did not want her to climax before him, neither did he want her to climax after him; he wanted them to reach their climax together. He pulled his tongue and finger out of her and whipped out his hard dick.

He was so filled with desire for this woman that he could not gradually thrust his dick inside her. Had it not been for her loud shriek, he would not have noticed that he had plunged his full length inside her. He pulled out of her, and tried to be gentle with his next couple of thrusts. But her pussy was so warm and inviting that, yet again, he got lost in his desires and was now thrusting his dick with all his might inside her.

He wanted to give her a taste of what a real man had to offer. Her husband was a fool for ever wanting more woman than her. Now, as they were making love, he knew that he definitely wanted more with this beautiful, sexy, love goddess. Yes, love goddess! He figured that she was not the type of woman who allowed men to hit it and quit it.

He was now panting as his hard dick slammed in and out her wet pussy. She was moaning out loud, calling his name, begging him not to stop. He could feel her fingers digging into his bare back as she licked her lips and took deep breaths to help her accommodate his long rod. She was amazing. Her body was amazing, and somehow, her pussy was latching onto his dick, making it hard to pull out. As he felt this tight grip on his dick, he almost went crazy and the momentum of his thrusts increased. She was now crying out with pleasure as he fucked her with every ounce of strength that he had, focusing on the thrusts of his dick. Their pleasure increased, and soon they both gave out a loud moan as they climaxed together, their juices exploding out of them. Exhausted from their lovemaking, they tried to cuddle in each other's embrace on her narrow couch. After what seemed like an hour, they recovered from their exhaustion, and once more, the strong attraction for each other lead them to another round of hot, passionate sex. This time, they went upstairs to the bed and appreciated each other's body one more time.

Months had gone by since their wild night of passion and Lilly and Carl had begun a more steady type of relationship. The sex that they shared was earth shattering and just the thought of Carl would sometimes get her wet. They would spend hours just making love to each other, using chocolate syrup, whipped cream, and whatever else they could get their hands on at the time. It had been a wild new type of love affair, different from what she had been used to with Perry. Although, it was scary at times for her because she could feel herself falling in love with this younger man and she was sure that he would probably not be the type to commit. Worst of all, she did not know whether she was ready to get herself into another committed relationship after what she had been through with Perry.

Speaking of Perry, he had now refused to sign the divorce papers, stating that if she wanted a divorce so bad, she should go ahead and do it herself. He had also made several attempts to apologize to her and got her to take him back, but this time she was done. She would not be able to handle it if she was to take him back and he cheated again. The best thing she could do was walk away from the situation and move on with her life.

Lilly had grown up in a single-parent home, with her mother working night and day to feed her and her sisters. She had first-hand experience of what a lack of having a father figure could do to a young girl. She had two beautiful little girls and never in a million years did she ever want to put them through a divorce, but Perry had made things impossible for her with his infidelity. She would have loved to try and make her marriage work, if he had not been cheating every time she took him back.

Meanwhile, Carl had been an excellent lover and friend, but she was not sure whether he would be there for the long haul. She had no relationship with her dad. She had only gone to visit him one time in Canada, where he was from, and she definitely knew that she wanted someone who would be committed to her and her kids. She feared that Carl would not be that type of guy. He was still discovering himself and she was sure he would not want the added responsibility of a family and kids.

As she made her way to his office, she decided that it was time they discussed their relationship and where it was going. She opened the front door and walked up to the guy at the reception desk. "Thank God, he did not have a woman working with him," she said to herself as she asked to see Carl. She swiftly made her way to his office, gently tapping on the door two times, before she heard his familiar voice asking her to come in.

"We need to talk, Carl," she said as she made her way to his desk. He stopped her dead in her tracks, as his extended arm pulled her in to meet him. He immediately, without warning, planted a passionate kiss on her lips. He continued to ravish her with his hot tongue. She melted at the feel of his touch on her skin, and she almost forgot why she had come to see him. She tried to open her mouth to explain the reason for her visit, but he did not allow her, again engaging her lips in a series of hot wet kissed that had her knees shaking.

His hand soon began roaming all over her body. Finally, she felt the cool breeze of the air in his office on her breast and realized that in the heat of the moment he had unbuttoned her blouse. She allowed him to further slip her clothes off as he whipped out his already erect dick.

His strong arms lifted her and placed her

seated on the end of his large, wooden desk. His dick soon found its way between her legs, and with one thrust he had his hot long cock inside her pussy. She had never been so engulfed by her desires for him, and she found herself moaning all sorts of crazy things, "Yeah, baby... Oh yeah... Muda-fucker... Oh shit, fuck me... Yes fuck!!" She had never been so verbal with her feelings. She felt free, and she was fully aroused and wanting more. She stopped him for a brief moment and got down on her knees. She used her mouth and took hold of his dick without using her hands. With one long, wet suck, she began her vicious attack on his dick with her tongue. She was going to drive him crazy with her tongue. She flicked her tongue back and forth on the head of the dick. His dick was long and full of body, there were a few small short veins running along it, and the head was big and pink.

"Oh yeah, Lilly... Don't stop... Just like that." He groaned as he now had his hand clasping the back of her head, controlling her every motion. She sucked his dick the way she had seen porn stars doing it on a video, and he was actually losing his balance as she now had full control of his body. He groaned over and over, as she lavished her tongue all over his huge cock. When she had enough, she got up and sat back at the tip of his desk with her legs parted. "Now fuck me, Carl," she instructed with a wicked smile on her face. He was all too pleased to do as she had instructed. He took his dick and plunged it over and over in her pussy, causing her to jerk back and forth on the desk with every thrust.

Over and over, he penetrated her insides with his mighty tool. Finally, they had an earth-shattering climax that she could have sworn penetrated the wall of his office.

"I had a confession to make," Carl said, as they were busy putting on their clothes and trying to tidy up from their moment of passion. Lilly looked at him with curious eyes, scared to death that it might be his way of breaking up with her. "I love you, and I want to be with you," he continued.

"I love you and want to be with you, too," she replied to him with a smile on her face.

He pulled her into him and whispered softly. "No Lilly, you don't understand. I love you and want to be with you. As in settle down with you and hopefully make you my wife," he added. It was at the moment that it dawned on Lilly. She had been so hurt by what she had experienced with Perry that she had not realized that Carl was falling in love with her.

"I really do love you Carl," she said, with a look of sincerity in her voice that made Carl confirm that she was definitely not the one night stand type of girl.

"Besides, it's about time I settle down," Carl continued. "And it's time for you to throw away this ring of thorns." he added, as he gently removed her wedding band from her finger and tossed it into the bin next to his desk. Lilly did not protest. She did agree that it was definitely time to move on with her life.

3 HER SECRET CRUSH

She felt like she could not breathe, and she was suddenly becoming nauseous and dizzy at the same time. As Anna looked around, she faced blurring visions of her peers throwing bananas and empty cupped at her. "FAT ANNA! FAT ANNA!" They shouted at the top of their lungs as they threw at her whatever they could get their hands on. Anna felt like she was in a small box that kept getting smaller and smaller. Finally, she dropped down to her knees and passed out.

When she woke up, she was lying on a bed. When she looked up, she saw Nurse Brown by the sink washing her hands. She got up and sat at the end of the bed, as she tried to remember how she got into the nurse's office.

Nurse Brown heard the crunching of the bedsprings, turned around, and walked over to her. "How are you feeling, Anna?" She asked, in a concerned mothering tone.

"I am doing ok. My head just hurts a little," Anna touched her head only to realize that she had a small bandage on the side of her forehead.

"For a minute there, you scared us. You fainted in the gym room. Your coach was late for class and, from what Nick told us, the other kids were making fun of you when you collapsed to the floor," said Nurse Brown. Anna recalled what happened and was embarrassed when hearing the nurse recount the story.

"Nurse Brown, could I please go home for the rest of the day? I'll be ok." She said, as she tried to get off the bed and leave this uncomfortable situation.

"Anna, you don't have to feel bad," the nurse assured her. "Bullying was something we took very seriously here at Creston." She informed Anna that an emergency PTA meeting had been called, and they would need her to cooperate so that they could help her. Anna's mom had been called in and was on her way. She could leave with her mother if she wanted.

A few minutes later, there was a knock at the door. When the nurse opened it, Anna's mom rushed in and hugged her daughter tightly. "Everything's gonna be ok, baby," she said, as she kissed her daughter on the forehead. "The nurse told me what happened."

She looked over to the nurse and shared some angry words about how the school was responsible for letting Anna's peers got away with bullying her. For some time she had made formal complaints to the principal, but no effective measures were taken. The most that was ever done was a token effort with no consequence; the students had been called in and asked to apologize to Anna.

But now that her daughter had suffered such humiliation to the point of having fainted, Shandra wanted these students punished.

"What time was the meeting with the parents?" She asked, as she was leaving the office with her daughter.

"It's at five, tomorrow," the nurse replied. Shandra stormed out of the nurse's office and headed to her car. On her way, she could see the evil stares of the children, as they looked on curiously. Some were trying to find out what had happened while others laughed secretly. The entire walk to the car was uncomfortable and horrible. Although no words were said out loud to them, the looks and the murmurs were emotionally vicious. She knew that this place and the way that her daughter was being treated for her weight, was very hurtful.

Anna Daniel was a slightly overweight fourteen-year-old. She had big brown eyes and a pretty round face. Her hair, never touched by chemicals, had a soft wavy texture; it was black in color, a few shades darker than her rich dark-chocolate complexion.

Her mother, Shandra, was a short, stout woman who wore thick, long, natural braids in her hair. She, too, was slightly overweight and had struggled all her life, because of her weight. Now, her daughter was going through the same things. The kids at the school did not care about her daughter's feelings; they enjoyed teasing and bullying her. They would call her all sorts of mean names, like "Fat Anna" and "Black Anna." She would come home crying, and it was only recently Anna had informed her mom of what had been happening at school. She did not want to got her mother involved for fear that they might tease her more and call her a big baby.

The only person she felt she could confide in was her best friend, Nick. He, too, was a little chubby. However, oddly enough, most people never bullied him, because of his "tough-boy" persona. Also, because he had a popular elder brother named Terrence who was in the twelfth grade. Terrence was not to be messed with. In fact, there was a rumor that he had spent a night in jail for punching the librarian when he was caught talking loud in the library. One thing Nick never got teased for was his complexion. He had a smooth tanned tone from his Caucasian mother and Hispanic dad.

There was also one other person who never teased her. He lived right next door. His name was Marcus, and he was Anna's secret crush. His mom worked with Anna's mom at the clinic. Every morning, their moms carpooled together, leaving Anna and Marcus sitting in the back seat together. Sometimes, they would talk about something on TV, or something that happened at their school, since they attended different schools.

However, he was in the twelfth grade, and he had a girlfriend, Suzie. Anna thought he was so handsome. He looked like "Prince Charming" from the Cinderella storybook she liked to read when she was a little girl. He had a gorgeous, dark complexion just like hers, and his hair was clean-cut with waves. He was tall, muscular, matured early, and he looked like he could be in his twenties. He had the most beautiful smile, and anytime she was daydreaming, it was about him. His smile would melt her heart. Even the sound of his voice made her heart race. Although she was just fourteen and did not know much about love, from the little she had heard, she was sure that what she felt for him was a rare, deep "happily ever after" kind of love. He never made fun of her size. In fact, they would joke and laugh about her weight in a good way. He was very funny, and he would always cheer her up with one of his jokes when she felt down.

Anna lived with her mom, in Arcadia, Louisiana. Her dad lived in the Bronx, New York, and she never really got to spend any time with him, or talk to him. However, when they got home that evening, the first thing her mom did was call him. She informed him of all the stuff that she had been going through, because of her size and her darker complexion.

When her dad spoke, he sounded very worried.

"I don't like what I'm hearing, Anny," he said. He normally called her "Anny," instead of Anna. "Hey, you wanna come stay over here with me, in the Bronx? There's lots to do over here, you know. Schools were great, and you could make new friends easily," he said, trying to convince her to go along with the idea before pitching it to her mother.

"Umm, not really," she replied unenthusiastically. "But I'll think about it." They spoke for almost an hour before she handed the phone back to her mother. Walking back to her room, she could hear her mother arguing on the phone about something, because she kept raising her voice to shout before finally hanging up the phone. When her mom came back to her room, she told Anna that her father thought that it would be a good idea for her to stay with him, to get away from all of what had been happening with them in Louisiana.

Although Shandra was sad, she had to admit that it could actually be a good thing for Anna to change environments. "Ok, let's make a deal," Shandra said, with tears in her eyes. "You finish high school here, and then, you could go to New York to go to college over there. If you want, that is," she continued. Anna did not mind going to New York for college. She had actually been researching colleges outside of Louisiana.

It may be a good idea to move to New York, she thought to herself. "Ok, yeah. I don't mind," she replied to her mom. "But stop crying, mom. I'm not leaving now," she laughed and grabbed a tissue to share.

The following day, Anna did not want to stay back for the PTA meeting, but Principal Greyson encouraged her to stay back.

"You need to tell their parents what they did to you. That's when these parents will take bullying seriously," he told her. It was soon time, and the parents seated themselves around the room. Anna stood outside and waited for Mr. Greyson to come out to get her and her mom, so they could address the other parents.

After a few minutes, he popped his head out of the door and asked them to come in.

They walked in slowly and stood in front of the class next to Mr. Greyson. He looked at Anna directly and asked her to explain what had happened the afternoon before in gym class.

"Well, I was heading to class, and when I changed into my shorts and T-shirt, all the other students started laughing and throwing stuff at me."

Mr. Greyson cut in, before she could continue and said, "Anna, tell us why they were laughing and throwing stuff at you."

"Because I'm...." She paused as she tried to fight back the tears that were now running down her cheeks. "I'm..."

"Go on, Anna, tell us why they felt that it was ok to throw stuff at you. Did you do anything to them?" Mr. Greyson looked closely at her.

"No, I did not do anything," she replied sadly. "They did it because I'm... I'm fat!" She finally spat it out and burst into tears. Her mom hugged her closely and then addressed the other parents.

"For years now, my daughter had been bullied by the other students because of her weight. They had taken her lunch money. They had thrown stuff at her. Some of them even spit on her." She said coldly. "For what? She had not done anything to none of them kids."

"They've been doing this because she was a little bigger than they were. C'mon people, look at me, I'm not skinny. She got it from me. We are not skinny people. We're a little bigger than most of you, but did that mean that we should be treated differently," she continued.

Mr. Greyson interrupted, again, and said that the school had a zero tolerance policy on bullying and violence. And that any student, or students, caught in the act would face punishment, which could include suspension and expulsion from school.

"This young girl fainted, people. She fainted, because of all the bulling that was done to her by her peers." He continued. "Thank you Anna, for sharing what happened with us. You may take a seat," he said, and pointed out two empty chairs that Anna and her mom could use to get seated. He ended the meeting saying, "Now, I had a list of names of the students who had been constantly harassing this poor girl. If your son's or daughter's name was on the list, please see me in my office privately."

The parents sat there in disbelief. None of them were proud of what the students had been doing to Anna. They circulated the list around, and the few of them whose children's names were not on the list left the room, while the others stayed back to speak with the principal.

Anna and her mom left and, on their way home, Shandra complimented her daughter on her bravery and speaking up. That night, they had stopped off at Applebee's for dinner, and Anna got to order her favorite entrée and dessert, a chocolate-chip ice cream sundae.

When they got home, Anna spent the entire evening talking to her best friend Nick online. He was not at the PTA meeting, but his mom had been there, and she had told him how some of the parents were upset at the children for their behavior towards her. Nick was the only person, apart from her mom, that really understood her.

He was always so supportive of her. They would spend hours talking online. She told him about going to college in New York, but he really wanted her to go to LSU in Shreveport, Louisiana, with him. It was the college that her mom had graduated from and Nick's sister was currently in college there. They continued chatting, and by the end of the night, he told her that whatever decision she makes, when she's ready to go to college, he would support her. It was about eleven in the night when they decided to go to bed.

After the emergency PTA meeting, the parents were now aware of the situation at the school, and most of them punished their children. The days after the meeting, Anna noticed a change in the behavior of her peers, but it was not a warm attitude. The ambience at the school was cold and hostile towards her. Although they did not throw stuff at her, or call her names, they gave her horrible stares and a cold shoulder. The only people that would speak to her were her teachers, and her best friend Nick. She still felt like she was being bullied. They were still being mean to her, without using words. She longed for the day when she would leave that school. She now actually looked forward to moving to New York.

Her graduation day was the best day of her life. She already had her bags packed and had already received the acceptance letter from the college in New York she would be attending. She would be travelling to New York on Friday afternoon to meet her dad. Her mom would stay back here in Louisiana, but would travel to see her while she was over there. She would be spending the first semester on campus so that she could really experience college life. However, after that semester, she would continue staying with her dad and his wife, in their apartment, which was about an hour away from campus.

The flight from the Shreveport International Airport, Louisiana, to La Guardia Airport, New York, was about four hours non-stop. Anna was greeted at the airport by her dad and his wife, Lisa. New York was everything she had dreamed it would be. It was so different from her hometown, Arcadia. There was a mixture of people from all different races and cultures. She could see black people, white people, Latinos, and Asians. Back in Arcadia, there were mostly black and white people, and it was a small town where the people knew each other.

Her father explained the whole subway transport system to her on their way from the airport. He told her that most people use the subway trains or buses to travel, instead of using cars. Anna was excited to get on the subway; this would be her first time riding the train. She had read about riding on trains in books and had seen people rushing to catch the train in movies, but she had never experienced any of these things herself. She looked around as they drove, and she marveled at the Sky Scrapers outside her window. They were huge, and the people who were going in and out of them were mostly dressed in black, gray, and blue suits.

When they got to the apartment, her father, Michael, told her that she could get settled in and spend the next two months with them, since the fall semester was starting in August and it was still early June. He had planned to take her around the city to just spend some quality time with his daughter. Anna's parents were married when she was a little girl, and she remembered how much fun she would have playing in the back yard with her dad. However, they got divorced when she was about seven, and she remembers it like it was yesterday. One evening, while they were having dinner, her parents told her that they were going to live in separate homes. They told her that they both loved her very much, and she was the most important thing in both of their lives. Her dad said he would be moving back to New York where he was born, and her mom would stay in Arcadia with her. He said that he would come down to Arcadia to visit her and she could also come to New York to visit him. "It's gonna be fun, you will get to travel a lot," she remembered him saying. This could not have been further from the truth. The divorce was the worst thing that happened to her family. Her dad only came to visit her about three times, and this was the first time she was traveling to see him. They would talk on the phone a few times a month and the father–daughter relationship that she once had with him changed. Talking to him was like talking to a distant relative, like an uncle that lived overseas in another country. Nonetheless, she was happy to be with him now and looked forward to spending this time with him and rebuilding their relationship.

The following day after she arrived, she went shopping with Lisa, her father's twenty-something-year-old wife. Lisa was more of a girlfriend figure than a stepmother. She took her to the trendiest stores at the mall, and they had pizza and ice cream for lunch. Overall, she enjoyed their little shopping extravaganza.

When they got home, she called her mom, to check in with her and see how she was doing. They both missed each other dearly. They had never spent this much time away from each other. She could tell from her mother's tone of voice that her mother was worried about how she was adjusting to life in the big city. "Okay honey! Well, just be careful and stay true to yourself, I love you." Her mother said as they ended their conversation.

"I promise I will. I love you too, and take care Mom," she replied and hung up the phone as she made her way to the computer to log into her Yahoo Messenger, to see if her best friend was online. She had not spoken with him since arriving here, and she knew that he probably missed talking to her. She was so happy to see him online. She spent the entire evening telling him about everything she had seen so far in New York. "You should come here, sometime, you'll like it, Nick," she said enthusiastically, as she continued to tell him how wonderful this place was.

Anna spent her summer going shopping with her stepmom, going to family barbeques, Coney Island, and trying to get a weight loss program that worked. After all the abuse she had suffered in high school, she was determined to lose the extra weight. She did not want to go into college looking the way she did.

She tried everything. She went on a fourteen-day cleanse diet, where she'd eat nothing all day and drank a mixture with maple syrup, cayenne pepper, and lemon juice. This diet made her so weak, but she was determined, and she got through fourteen days of what seemed like hell. However, when she got on the scale on the fifteenth day, she had only lost four pounds. This diet was supposed to make you lose at least one pound per day. It was a rapid weight loss technique.

She had been speaking to Lisa about her weight issues, and Lisa had suggested that she join a gym. "You know what, you could join the gym where I go," Lisa said. She looked at Lisa, and thought that she would definitely lose the weight now. Lisa was a physically attractive young lady. She was tall and slender, and she had the most perfect abs. "Yeah, I could definitely give your gym a try," Anna replied.

The following afternoon, Anna and her Lisa headed out to the gym wearing cotton leggings, tank tops, and sneakers. When they got to the gym, Lisa introduced Anna to her personal instructor, and soon, they began their usual workout together.

The workout was intense, and Anna felt like she would pass out. There was even a point where she felt like she could not breathe. She soon realized that these workouts at the gym may not be as easy as she thought it would be. They spent about two hours at the gym, and by the time they were done, Anna's body felt sore. She felt like she spent more than five hours there. When they got home, Anna rushed to take a quick shower and lay down for the rest of her evening. Her muscles were sore, and she could barely move them without clinching with pain. She dreaded going back to the gym a second time. That night, although she wanted to go online to tell Nick about her horrible experience working out at the gym, she was too tired to get off the bed. So, she decided that she would just tell him all about it tomorrow.

The next day at the gym was harder than

the first day. Her body was aching from the previous day, and she was trying to exercise while she was in utter pain. Although mentally, she knew that the reason she was in such pain was probably because the techniques were actually working, physically, her body could not take much more of these. When they left the gym that night, she decided to break the news to Lisa. Although she wanted to lose the weight, spending hours at the gym was not how she would do it. She did not even think she could survive another day of going to the gym.

Lisa tried to encourage her, and told her that her first couple of days working out would be tough, but she did not have to give up.

"I'm not giving up," she said, "I just need some time to relax and heal from these sore muscles," she continued. However, Anna did not return to the gym for the rest of the summer. Soon, the fall semester was upon her, and they were moving her stuff into a tiny dorm room on campus. Her dad had paid for the entire room, and therefore, she did not have a roommate. "Moving on campus is one thing, but dealing with a roommate is a whole other thing, trust me, I know what am saying," he told her. Anna had been an only child, and was used to having her own space. So she did not at all mind the fact that she had her own room, and did not have to share it with anyone else.

Getting her room ready was very hectic. They had to get her a microwave, a TV, a mini refrigerator, an ironing board and iron, a comforter set, and other stuff for her room. After they had done all that, she had to go register all her classes at the Intramural Centre. The lines were long when she got there, and she spent the entire day there, going back and forth from the admission counter to the place where she had a photo taken for her school ID badge, to the counter where she had to get her meal plan set up with the cafeteria, and finally, to the cashier window to pay for everything. When she was done with all of this, it was late in the evening and her dad had been in the room with Lisa setting everything up. By the time she was done doing everything and got back to the room, they were sitting on her bed watching TV. She told them how hectic it was completing the registration process. They offered to take her out to dinner now that she was a college girl. That night, when she got home, she took a quick shower and went to bed, forgetting to go online and tell Nick about her first day at college.

Anna had gotten really settled in at college, and she had begged her dad to let her spend her four years on campus. She would go home to visit him on weekends. She was now in her junior year, and it was going well. Her grades were well above average, and thankfully, it was nothing like high school. She had made several new friends while at college. The students here were more mature, and they did not make fun of her weight or her darker complexion.

However, she did still want to try to lose the weight, because while all of her friends were going out on dates, she was never once asked to go out on a date.

Could it be that, although they did not say it out loud or tease her about it, the students were still quite aware of her weight issue, and as a result the guys were not attracted to her? Anna longed desperately to go out on a date. She would be happy if anyone would ask her out. She did not really care what they would do on the date, it didn't even had to be anything fancy. She just wanted to feel attractive and wanted by a guy.

College was the time to go to school during the week and party during the weekends, but with her, it seemed like all she ever did was go to school and on weekends spend time at home. Anna was tired of this cycle that had been going on for years now.

Her weight problems had followed her into college, and she tried everything she could to lose the extra pounds. She tried all sorts of crazy diets, counting calories, exercising, and starving herself. However, nothing seemed to work. Anna was at a point where she was now researching liposuction. Had she found a way to get the money for the surgery she would have tried to get the procedure done. Her parents reassured her constantly that she was beautiful and she needed to accept her size, but Anna was not having it. She was determined to lose the weight or die trying.

One Thursday night, she sat watching television like she normally did every night after doing her homework. A commercial came on. It was for this new product called "Gone," which was a powder that you sprinkle over anything that you eat. This product was supposed to cut your appetite and also boost your metabolism, so you got energy and burned the calories that you took in quickly. This had to be one of the most ridiculous weight loss claims out there, she thought to herself, but at $1.99 a pack, she decided that it would not hurt to give it a try. The ad continued explaining what the product did, and it also spoke about the fact that their customers don't have to stick to any diet. They could continue eating like they normally did, and they would not have to do any intensive workouts.

This sounded too good to be true; this "miracle powder," which Anna referred to the product as, sounded like something she could do easily. "Wow, eat what I want, and don't exercise much," she thought to herself. As soon as the 1-800 customer service numbers came on the screen, she picked up her phone and called and placed an order. If it worked, that would be great, but if it did not work, that could be okay since she only spent about two dollars purchasing it.

It took about a week to get the package in the mail. Anna was excited when she received it. One of her girlfriends was with her when she opened the large brown envelope, which contained a pouch-like packet of the product. The instructions on the package were very straightforward. "Sprinkle a little "GONE" on everything you eat, and see the pounds melt off. In a few weeks, all the extra weight would be Gone."

They laughed when they read this line, but they were really curious to see whether this product would actually work. "Well, let me be the first to say, that's two dollars you just sent down the drain," her friend said.

"Yeah, I kind of got the feeling that I just got scammed," Anna replied, in a melancholy voice. Although she did not think that the product would work, she still decided to use it. So every time she was about to eat anything, she would sprinkle a little of the product on her food. She continued doing this daily, and after about three months, the packet was completely empty.

One day while out shopping with Lisa, Anna took her normal size sixteen pair of jeans into the dressing room to try. However, it fit very loosely. "This must be an extra-large size sixteen, Lisa," she said to Lisa, as she took out the pants to make sure she was putting on the right jean size. As she looks at the tag, she was almost certain that she had taken a size eighteen or twenty, but realized that it was in fact a size sixteen. She calls out to Lisa again and said, "these were some pretty big jeans, could you pass me a size fourteen." Lisa went back to the rack, and this time pulled out a size fourteen and a size twelve pair of jeans. She first handed Anna the larger size, but just as she had suspected, they were also too big, and so were the size twelve. Finally, she got Anna a size nine, and they fit perfectly. Lisa had noticed the weight loss, but she honestly thought Anna could see that she had lost a lot of weight. When Anna saw that the size nine fit her, she was shocked. She had never been a size nine for as long as she could remember.

Tears of joy streamed down her face. This was a surprising discovery. For years, she had struggled with her weight, and had tried everything to lose the extra pounds. Now, the product that she least expected to work, actually worked. During recent times, Anna did realize that most of her clothes were becoming very baggy, but she was so consumed with preparing for exams, that she barely paid any attention to the way her clothes looked on her. The first thing she did when she got home from the mall was call her mom, to share the good news with her.

After seeing the shocking results of her weight loss, Anna decided that she needs to do a whole body makeover. She began her day and heads to one of the most talked about hair salons there. She got her hair relaxed, and added blonde highlights. Before she left the salon, she got a manicure, pedicure, and her legs waxed. Leaving the salon, she could see herself in the mirror, and she had to admit to herself that she looked like a completely transformed person.

The only thing she was missing were some

new clothes, and she knew exactly who to call. Lisa met her at the mall in less than an hour, and she had her husband's credit card to use. They went from store to store, picking out the sexiest, most feminine, clothes they could find. They also bought some new heels and boots. When Anna went back to her room, she could hardly wait to show off her new clothes tomorrow, when she went to class.

When she entered the class, all the students were shocked. They had never seen her dressed like that before. Anna normally threw on a pair of jeans and a T-shirt and went to class with her hair in a ponytail. However today, her hair was straightened out, and it fell on her shoulders. She had beautiful blonde highlights in them, and it looked too perfect to be real. She was wearing a red, low-cut summer dress that was about an inch below her knees, with red fur boots.

As she entered the class, she could feel the stares of her classmates. For the first time, it was a positive stare. It was not a cold shoulder kind of stare, but rather, it was a warm inviting type of stare. She walked in and had a seat. Throughout the duration of the class, she received compliments on her new look from several of the guys in the class.

When class was over, one of the guys walked up to her and asked her out to the movies on the weekend. Anna's heart leaped with joy. "This would be my first date," she thought to herself. She was so excited she could hardly contain herself. The rest of her day went unspoiled as she anxiously waited for the weekend.

When she got home that evening, she told Lisa about her date and asked for her help in finding something nice to wear. Later on, she called her mother, Shandra, and told her all about her new makeover. She also told her about her first date. Shandra really wanted to be around for her first date, and she felt a little sad that she was missing out on such a special occasion for her daughter.

"Make sure you send me some pics," she said to her when they were about to end the call. Soon, it was the weekend, and Anna was getting ready to go out on her first date.

Although she was twenty-one, her dad was still very protective of her. He was even more anxious to meet her date. He had a list of questions in his head that he would ask this boy, to see if he was worthy enough to took his daughter out on her first date.

Anna was still upstairs with Lisa getting ready when he heard the knock on the door. "Anna, Lisa, he's here," he yelled, as he went to open the door. The young guy's name was Dereck, but before he could grill Dereck with all of his questions, his daughter came downstairs to meet her date. She looked beautiful. She was going to the movies. Yet, she was wearing an outfit that made it seem like she was going out to dinner at a fancy restaurant.

"Be careful, honey," her father said as he watched his daughter leave the apartment to go out on her first date. He tried hard to ignore the fact that he was not fond of this young man. He had his hair braided, and he wore a stud in one ear. He was also dressed in jeans and a T-shirt.

This guy put very little into making a good impression, and he was not sure if he would want his daughter to go out on a second date with someone like that. "C'mon relax, honey. It's just a movie. She's a big girl, she can handle herself," Lisa said, as she came over and gave him a hug to comfort him.

The movie that they watched was hilarious, and they laughed the entire time. However, Anna did not feel any connection to this guy. There was no spark between them. She reminisced about the times that she spent with her secret childhood crush, and wondered if this was how it would be if they were to meet again and go out on a date. "That would really suck," she thought to herself, as they walked out of the cinema after the movie.

Dereck was a gentleman and did not try to disrespect her or anything of the sort. They had a pleasant conversation on their way home, and when he dropped her off, he leaned in to give her a peck on the check.

After that date, she continued to see Dereck in class, but they never went out again. She figured that he, too, did not feel any chemistry between them. She continued going out on simple dates, on and off, but it was never really anything serious, and they never had sex.

Although she hated to admit it, she would

compare the guys to her childhood crush. When they did not meet all of her criteria, she would not even go out on a second date with them.

Soon, it was graduation day, and she was leaving college with a degree in accounting. Her mom had traveled to New York to be at her graduation, and the two of them would head back to Arcadia the next weekend. She would find a good job down there and got settled in again. After all, Arcadia was her hometown. Though she liked New York, she missed home. Anna spent her last week in New York taking her mom sightseeing and shopping. The week went by quickly, and soon, they were on a plane traveling back to her former hometown.

She pulled out the most provocatively sexy casual dress that she had in her suitcase when she got to the house. She sat it on the bed and planned how she would spend her next day in Arcadia. She decided that she would spend the day going out, around the town, to see what had changed over the years.

She also wanted to see her secret childhood crush, Marcus. She had been away for four years, and yet, she still remembered him and longed to see how much he had changed. When they got to the house, she asked her mom about him and his mom. She was told that they had moved to another part of Arcadia. She also learned that he no longer stayed with his mom. He had his own apartment and was currently in college. She was surprised, because she thought that he would have been graduating out of college around the same time as her. Anna had been saving herself for him, or someone similar to him. So, she was a little disappointed that he no longer lived next door. However, she decided to be hopeful. Arcadia was a small town, and people were constantly bumping into each other. So, she was sure that she would see him around.

There was a knock at her door. When she opened her eyes, and glanced over at the alarm clock on her nightstand, she realized that it was the following morning already. The clock showed that it was ten o'clock, and she got up to answer her bedroom door.

Her mom stood there on the phone talking. "Well I would not be too worried about that," Shandra was finishing off her conversation. Her mom then handed her the phone saying, "Oh I am sorry Anna, it's your call." Anna looked puzzled.

"Who is it?" She asked.

"It's Nick," her mom replied. Anna quickly grabbed the phone with excitement and rushed off to sit on her bed and chat with her friend. With everything that was going on with her life lately, she had grown distant from her best friend. It had been months since they last spoke on the phone, and although he knew she was coming home after graduation, he did not know the date she was returning.

Before they could greet each other, Anna began apologizing for not calling to let him know that she was back home. "How did you know I was here?" she asked him. "C'mon now, Arcadia is a small town. People talk," he said laughing. She breathed a sigh of relief.

She thought he would have been really upset with her and not want to talk to her again.

"Reallllyyy," she replied. They continued chatting for hours on the phone. They spoke about everything, life in New York compared to life in Arcadia, her graduation day, and her flight. They even spoke about Marcus. She had a great friendship with Nick, and he knew all of her secrets. When she first told him about her crush on Marcus, they were about twelve years old, and he had laughed at her.

As the years went by, he would sometimes make little funny comments about her imaginary relationship with Marcus. She had gotten to a point where she referred to Marcus as her future husband. She remembered one time, when she almost told Marcus that he was her future husband.

Nick told her that he had been thinking about going to college himself. After graduating from high school, Nick had gone to work with his father in their family restaurant. Although cooking was like an art form in his family, and he was a great cook, he wanted to be a well-qualified chef. He was in the process of deciding whether he wanted to travel to Miami, to study at one of highest ranking Culinary Arts Institutions or remain in Louisiana to study Restaurant Management.

Anna was very supportive of him. She advised him that he should do whatever his heart desired, even if it meant leaving home and going somewhere new. Working at the restaurant was very hectic. He barely had any free time this week, but next week, he had a few days off. So, they planned to see each other on the following Tuesday. After a while, they finally ended their call and looked forward to meeting the following week.

The next few days in Arcadia, Anna was shocked to see the amount of attention she got from men whenever she went out. The men were practically throwing themselves at her, single and married men. She had received several date offers, but none seemed to interest her. Maybe she was a hopeless romantic, but she wanted Marcus, and nobody else. Her mom was encouraging her to go out on at least one date and had fun.

She spent her days job hunting, shopping, or just laying around the house sometimes, watching TV. She had a degree in accounting. Yet, she was not making any money. It was Sunday morning, and as they were entering the church, there he stood, more handsome than ever. Marcus was standing outside church talking with his cousin, Leroy, when Anna's eyes caught sight of him from the car, when they pulled up in the parking lot.

He had not changed much. He looked like a male model. He stood up straight with his shoulders up high, giving off a confident look in his black suit. She could see him smiling from the distant. As she got out of the car to walk over to the church, she could feel butterflies in her stomach. Her knees were shaking and her heart was pounding. She was suddenly very self-conscious. "Oh God, I hope I don't trip and fall," she kept thinking to herself, as she drew closer and closer to where he stood.

When Marcus saw her, he had to look hard before he could recognize her. "Hi Marcus," she said, when she got next to him.

"Anna, is that you?" he said in disbelief. She nodded her head shyly.

"How you been, girl?" he said, as he gave her a big hug. At that moment, Anna was officially the happiest young woman alive. She felt her heart stop for a second, as he embraced her. She tried to maintain her composure and not act overly excited.

"When did you get back?" he asked her. She told him that she had gotten back a few days ago. They then walked away from his cousin to a quiet corner on the side of the church. "You look amazing, I could hardly recognize you," he continued and he complimented her on every part of her body.

The entire time, Anna felt like she was in heaven. He asked her about life in New York and why she decided to come back home. She asked him about his life and what he had been up to these days. He told her that after he graduated from high school he spent a few years working, doing little odd jobs, like painting, plumbing, and carpentry.

He had always been a very manual, hands-on kind of guy, but he realized that these things don't guarantee you work through the year.

So, he went to college. He was now in his second year of law school. She told him that she was happy that he decided to go back to school, stating that he did the smart thing. After a while, the conversation came easily, and they arranged to meet up that evening for dinner and to catch up some more.

The entire time she was in the church, Anna kept secretly looking at him from the corner of her eyes. She was so excited about tonight. This would be her first date with him. In fact, this would be her dream date. The rest of the day seemed to go by slowly. It was finally seven o'clock, and she was all dressed up and waiting for him to come pick her up.

She wore a tight, figure-hugging, mini black dress that was so short she couldn't even bend over in it without exposing the red, lacy thong underwear that she had been saving for a night like this one.

She had a pair of six-inch peep toes with a bow on the front part of it. When she heard the knock at the door, her heart skipped with joy. She knew that it was Marcus. She leaped forward to get the door. Her mom was there with her. Shandra was excited for her daughter. She had known that Anna had a crush on Marcus from way back in the days, when she would carpool with his mother. When Shandra opened the door for him, he was very polite to her. He seemed to be the perfect gentleman. He presented Anna with a red rose, and they headed out on their first date.

The restaurant that they went to was very classy, and the food there was phenomenal. They had some good laughs at the dinner table, and they really enjoyed each other's company. He invited her to his apartment afterwards, so that they could have some wine and talk some more. He had a small, one-bedroom apartment that was a few blocks down from campus. When they got there, he asked her to get comfortable. Then he pulled out a bottle of wine that he said he had been saving for his graduation.

They sat on the couch next to each other, and they were having fun drinking the red wine and talking to each other. After a while, she began feeling sensations within her. They weren't like anything she had felt before. Anna had a few beers in the past, but had never sat and drunk almost half a bottle of red wine. She had gotten tipsy off of the red wine.

She looked over at him, and he looked like the most gorgeous man she had ever seen. She leaned over and gently placed her lips on his. Their lips locked together, and they began kissing feverishly. She wanted more of him, and as they kissed, all the longing that she was holding back for all these years began manifesting itself. He did not resist her. He was just as horny for her, and his kisses were full of desire as well.

Anna drew closer to him, and he began panting hard as she began kissing his neck with her hot desperate lips. He moaned from the pleasure, and his hands roam freely all over her breasts. He finally found the zipper in the back of the dress, as he focused his attention on keeping her lips warm with his and getting her out of her dress at the same time. He was finally able to pull the dress off her shoulders, and her breasts bounced out of place. She was not wearing a bra. He pulled back his lips from hers and launched a sensual attack on her nipples. He licked them and sucked them one by one. She moaned out loud at the touch of his tongue on her tiny black nipples. "Oh God," she moaned as she flung her hair back and tried to relax, as he drove her wild with his wicked tongue. She had her eyes closed and was enjoying the moment, until she felt the pressure of his finger trying to penetrate its way into her pussy. "Ouch," she said as she stiffened.

It was then that Marcus realized that this girl was untouched by any other man. She was a virgin. The very thought of that made his penis throb even harder with desire. He had never had sex with a virgin, but it had always been a fantasy that he longed to experience. He knew that he had to be gentle with her, or else she might make him stop, and he would have a serious case of blue balls.

He gently picks her up and carries her to his room. He was not about to take her virginity on this couch. This was a special occasion, and the least he could do, considering her tipsy state, was deflower her on a bed. She could feel that she was being carried away, and she then felt pillows. She knew that she was in his room. Although she was scared, she had always wanted Marcus, and she had dreamed of her first time being with him. As she lay down on the bed, he spread her legs and was about to put his lips on her pussy. "Wait," she said, and looks down at him. He pulled his head up and looks at her.

"I've never done this before," she said embarrassed.

"Don't worry, I'll be gentle. You'll enjoy this, trust me baby," he replied, and kissed her softly on her stomach. He then proceeded to go back to what he was about to do before she interrupted him. He used his fingers and gently rubs against her clitoris. "You like this?" he asked her.

"Yesss," she moaned, as she enjoys the sensations that result from his finger movements.

"Good," he replied, as he went down between her legs and used his tongue to gently lick her clitoris. He then took the clitoris into his mouth and sucked it. Then, he used his tongue and flicked it back and forth along the pink insides of her pussy.

"Mmm," she moaned, as her juices begin flowing down into her pussy. This was the sweetest feeling that she had ever felt. It was much better than the butterflies that she used to get in her stomach. She grabbed his hair, as she twisted and turned her body trying to get an even greater sensation. His licked intensify, and he began to suck a little harder. Her pussy was now slippery wet, and he knew that she was ready for him.

He pulled his dick out of his pants and in an instant, without warning, he tried to stick it into her pussy.

"Ouch," she said as her body stiffens from the sudden pain.

"Just relax, baby," he said, as he went down between her legs again, and sucked her clitoris again. Once more, he took his hard dick, and this time, he gently tried to penetrate it inside her. He rubbed it back and forth along her pussy hole like he was trying to find an opening to thrust it into. He increases the force of his penetration. "Oh, oh," she moaned in pain, as she gripped his arms tightly. The pain was intense, and she felt like someone was stabbing her with a knife in the most sacred, untouched part of her body.

He looked into her eyes and told her, "C'mon baby, you can do this. Let me have you. Please, I need you."

As he was talking to her, he was penetrating inside her pussy with his dick. He continued to thrust inside her. He, too, was now moaning.

"Stop, please stop," Anna cried out.

"I'm almost there, my love. Just let me go on. It's going to be all good, I promise," he reassures her, and continued to push his dick further inside her extremely tight pussy.

He pulled out of her pussy and, with a mighty thrust, went back in. "OOO," she yelled, as he looked down at her. He kissed her on her forehead. "I'm all in now," he said, as he now began to thrust repeatedly inside her.

Gradually, all the pain that Anna was feeling subsided. These feelings were now replaced with the previous sensations that she was feeling when he was licking her pussy.

Her moans were sounds of pleasure, and her body movements begin to synchronize with his movements. "Oh this is sweet," he moaned, as his energies all channelled into the stroke of his manhood.

Anna had never felt anything like this before in her life. There was no more pain, and she could feel tiny shock waves going through her body with every stroke. His thrusts were long and hard, then changed.

He held onto the pillow that she had her head on, and his thrusts become harder and more intense. Anna closed her eyes and loses herself to the sensations. Her pussy was now controlling her thoughts and actions. She felt this ecstasy running through her body, and her moaning increases as his sweat drops down on her bare skin. He was ramming into her so hard that the bed was jolting forward with every thrust. He was moaning louder and louder as he fucked her. He groaned then began sucking on her neck as he penetrated inside her. That almost drove her crazy. She moaned even louder than him. "Yes... Oh yes," she screamed, as she felt like she was about to climax. There was an explosion inside her. He could not hold back.

His cum drips out of her pussy, while his dick was still inside her. She held onto his butt and now brings her pussy up towards him. Her clitoris was rubbing against his groin. She, too, reaches her climax, and a loud moan escapes her lips while her body drops down onto the bed. They were both exhausted, and they look at each other with glow on their faces. Although tipsy, Anna knew exactly what had happened, and she was content.

They spoke for a while after. Anna confessed that she had always had a crush on him growing up. Marcus was surprised. He had no idea that she liked him when they were children. After a while, they got up off the bed, and he got ready to take her home.

The ride home was nice and quiet. There were not many cars out, and the moon was shining bright. It was a perfect night. When she got home, it was about one in the morning. As she walked in, she realized that her mom had fallen asleep, waiting for her on the couch. She ran upstairs not wanting to wake her up. The first thing she did was turn on her computer.

She wanted to call Nick to tell him about her evening, but she decided that he might be asleep. So she went online to see if he was still up. When she saw he was online, she was so happy. She told him all about her evening. "It was the perfect date. He was such a gentleman. I couldn't believe I finally did it, and it was with him. OMG, I can't believe this," she typed in the conversation box. Although Nick was unhappy about the entire situation, he tried to remain positive for her. He encouraged her to be careful, because most guys could not be trusted.

They went to bed after about an hour of chatting, since it was really late. That night, Anna was so happy and excited that she could hardly sleep. She kept reminiscing about the events of the evening. "Oh, what a wonderful night," she thought to herself, as she lay in her bed watching the ceiling fan in her room spin.

The following day when Anna woke up, the first thing she did was check her cell phone to see whether she had any missed calls from Marcus. There were no missed calls. She whispered a little prayer saying, "Dear God, please. I never asked for much, but please let Marcus call me. Please!"

She got out of bed and proceeded to start her day. Her phone rang while she was having breakfast downstairs. She nearly fell off her seat with excitement when she saw Marcus pop up on the caller ID. She immediately answered the call. "Hello," she said, trying to sound as calm as possible.

Marcus had called her alright. He had just called her to remind her that she needed to pick up some Morning-after pills at the pharmacy, since he had ejaculated inside her pussy. Although Anna remembered most of the stuff that happened that night, she had never realized that he had ejaculated inside of her.

She sprung off the chair and headed to the store immediately, to buy the pills. If there was one thing she knew she did not want to deal with right now, was a baby. During the entire drive to the store, she kept thinking how she could have been so careless. She should have ensured that they were using protection. Once she got the pill in her hands, she purchased a bottle of water right there at that store, and took the pill on her way out.

She did not want any accidental pregnancy that was the result of a hot night of passion.

She called Marcus to let him know that she had just taken the pill, and he had nothing to worry about. On that same call, she told him she had really enjoyed her evening with him, and she would love to go out again some other time. Marcus politely informed her that he was busy right at the time, but he would call her later to arrange another date. She waited for this call the entire day, but he never called her.

When she got up the next day, the alarm on her phone went off. It was a reminder that she was having lunch with Nick at twelve-thirty. She checked to see whether she had any missed calls from Marcus, but once again, she was disappointed when she saw that he had not called her.

She decided that she would give him a call a little later in the morning and called him at about eleven. When she reminded him that he said he would call her back yesterday, he told her that he did call her, but she never picked up.

"You did? That's odd. I did not receive any of your calls. For a minute there, I thought you were trying to avoid me," she said with a little chuckle.

"No, of course not," he replied. They spoke for a while on the phone, and they arranged a second date, but this time, it was a movie night over at his apartment.

Twelve-thirty was soon upon her, and she walked into the small café briskly trying to locate Nick. He was not there, so she called his phone. At a distance, she saw this handsome-looking guy picking up his phone. "Hello."

It was Nick's voice on the other end of the phone. Her eyes nearly popped out of its sockets when she realized how much he had changed. He was no longer chubby. He had a thin mustache and had matured into a good-looking young man. Similar to her, he had transformed, and he looked like a completely different person.

It had been four years since she had seen him, and she was impressed with his new looks. "Nick," she said, as she walked over to where he was seated.

He looked up at her, and from the look in his eyes, she could tell that he, too, was amazed at how she had changed her appearance. She had her hair pulled back in a ponytail, and she wore a medium-length white summer dress with a pair of pink and white wedge heels. They had a lovely lunch, where they talked and talked about everything.

Later on in the evening, as she lay in her bed alone, she decided to give Marcus a call. She could had sworn she heard him pick up and then end the call when she said, "Hello." She tried calling again, but the phone was now switched off, and the call went directly to his voicemail.

She did not quite understand what to think of this, but she decided to call Nick instead, and see what he was up to. He was watching a movie on TV.

"What station is it on?" she asked him. When he told her the station number, she took the remote and put her TV on the same station. They watched the movie and talked on the phone at the same time, laughing at various scenes. It was almost like they were at the movies together. When the movie was over, they talked some more and finally when it was almost midnight. They decided to say goodnight and go to bed.

When she woke up again, Anna checked her phone to see if she had any missed calls from Marcus. There were no missed calls from him, as usual. They had planned to watch a movie at his apartment tonight, but here he was not calling her.

She decided to give him a call. Surprisingly, he answered his phone. Once again, he was very polite, and said that he had been busy when she called. He also told her that he would be busy tonight as well.

However, he wanted her to come over around one, so they could watch the movie. Anna was thrilled at the opportunity to get to spend time with him again. She jumped at the idea and even offered to bring snacks with her. "Cool, can't wait," she said excitedly, as they got off the phone.

As she knocked on the door of his apartment, a negative thought crossed her mind. "What if he had a girlfriend," she thought. However, she tried to brush off that thought.

When he opened the door, wearing nothing but a pair of boxer shorts, she could not even remember what she had been thinking about. She walked in, and they sat on the couch together.

"Excuse my manners," he said. "It's so hot in here, I had to strip down. Hope you don't mind," he continued. "Oh sure, I'm cool with that," Anna replied.

He had an amazing body, and she was turned on at the sight of him with barely any clothing on. He stood up and invited her to join him to his shelf on the wall, where he kept his DVD collection. "I'm not sure what you like, so, you could pick whichever movie you want." He said to her.

Anna got up off the couch where she had been sitting, and walked over to the shelf where he had his movies. He walked behind her, and she could literally feel his breath on her shoulder. She looked down and her eyes caught a glimpse of his erection through his boxers. He saw her watching it, and he pulled it out for her to see, "Whoa!" she exclaimed. The night when they made love, she hadn't really gotten the opportunity to look at his dick. But right now, she was having a close up with it.

His dick was long and hard, and the head was big and round. The dick, itself, had a slightly bent shape. Right away, she felt a strong attraction to his penis and had a burning desire to taste it. She slowly went down on her knees, cupped his dick with both her hands, and slowly sucked it. She sucked it again slowly, going down almost to the base of the penis with her mouth, then, slowly working her way up to its head. Marcus groaned. She looked up at him, as he tilted his head backwards and enjoys the sensations that he felt between his legs.

She began sucking his dick the way she would see the women do in the porn videos she had seen. She licked it with her tongue from the bottom up. Then, when she got to the head of the dick, she slowly traced the edges of the head with her tongue. Then, she flicked her tongue back and forth on the tip of the head. She could see that his knees were shaking, and he braces himself up against the wall. He opens his legs wider, so she could have more access to his manhood.

"Ooo," he groaned, as he closed his eyes and used his hand to grab hold of her head. He was now in control of her head movements on his dick, and he was shoving his dick inside her mouth. She also tightens her grip on his penis with her mouth, and sucked his dick long and hard. She could hear him panting right now. "Oh yes, baby... Baby... Yeah, suck it... Suck that big black cock," he said, as he continued to stab her in her mouth with huge cock. As she sucked his dick, she could feel it getting harder and longer and it was pulsating more and more. Finally, he moved her head off of his dick and grasped her to her feet.

In a swift movement, he turned her around, and her face was now against the wall. He had her hands stretched out holding onto the wall, as he entered her from behind. He could hardly believe how wet her pussy was. He began pushing his penis inside her tight pussy, and his thrust jolts her body upwards against the wall. He used one hand to pin her up against the wall, and the other to rub on her clitoris, pulling and rubbing against it.

"Uh huh, just like that. Yeah, it felt good," Anna moaned, as she now felt that stimulation on her clitoris, while being fucked like an animal up against the wall. Her ass was jiggling as he rams his dick inside her with the force of his body on her ass with his thrust. "Oh yeah, it's good," she said, as she enjoys the way he ravished her pussy from the back. His movements got faster and harder! "Uh, uh, uh!" She shrieked, as she felt the full extent of his dick inside her. He pulled back a little and grabbed her by her waist. She was no longer as close to the wall as she was before.

"Bend over," he told her. She bends over with her legs open and her ass popped out into the air. Her hands could touch her toes in this position. He was now about to really destroy her pussy. He grabbed her by her ass and slams his big, hard dick inside her. She shrieked in pain and pleasure. He gripped firmly onto her and continued to thrust his cock inside her pussy, while she screams out with unimaginable pleasure.

"Oh God, Oh GOD. I'm going to cum," he said with urgency in his voice. "O SHIT, MUDA FUCKER... damn, damn," he said, as he explodes inside her pussy. She, too, had climaxed with him, and her pussy was contracting as it spews out his cum and her cum together.

"Damn, girl, that was amazing," he said, as he smacks her on her ass.

"Really," she said, and turns around to look at him. He kissed her. This kiss was raw and full of passion. She almost lost balance. She was so caught up in this man that she had allowed him to cum inside her pussy again. "We really need to use a condom, the next time," she said. "You can't keep cumming inside me like that," she continued.

"Yeah, am sorry about that. I just kind of lost it in there. You could pick up some Plan B pills on your way home right?" He asked her in a tone that seemed more like he was instructing her to purchase the pills.

"Yeah, definitely," she replied. As she left the apartment that day, although she enjoyed their moment of passion, she had several unanswered questions in her mind. She picked up the morning-after pill, and took it immediately, fearing that she might have negative side effects of taking too much of the pill within such as short period of time. She went home and called Nick. She really needed to speak to her best friend to hear what his advice would be on her situation. This was beginning to seem like a friends without benefits type of relationship, where the men got sex from the women, without any commitments.

"I knew this would happen," Nick shouted angrily. Anna began thinking that she probably should not had told Nick about her suspicions about Marcus, because he was furious at her. "You know what, let me make a call and see what's up with this guy," he said.

Before Anna could try to convince him to stay out of the situation, he hung up the call. He called her back a few minutes later. "Anna, I knew something was up with Marcus. I should have listened to my gut feeling," he said coldly. "He's got a girlfriend. I just spoke to his cousin, and he and that girlfriend were supposedly really tight. Am sorry he had been playing you. That bastard had been playing you." He said, with anger and remorse in his voice. Anna could not believe what she was hearing. Her suspicions about Marcus were finally confirmed. She had been hoping that it was all in her head. She knew that Nick probably felt bad for not protecting her. But how? He hadn't really got the time to try to protect her.

She hopped into bed with Marcus at the first opportunity she got, because she had a silly childhood crush on him. She could not believe that she had found herself in this type of situation. How could he had been so deceitful towards her? She wanted to confront him, but she knew that he would probably just deny the whole thing. She did not know what to do.

Nick listened to her cry about her mistake, and he was comforting and non-judgmental the entire time. He told her that some men were just jerks at the end of the day, and the women that they lie to were just victims.

"C'mon Anna, everyone's a fool for love sometime," he said to her, as he tried to cheer her up. "Focus on getting a job, you know. Don't worry about that asshole. Be happy that, you know, you found out early." Anna knew he was just trying to be a supportive friend, and she appreciated his honesty, but she was feeling emotionally drained and just wanted to sleep it off and forget this ever happened. She regretted acting upon her feelings, and she wished that she had left things the way they were.

"Why did I have to go sleep with my secret crush?" She thought to herself, as she cried alone in her room. Nick came by her home to see her later that evening. He brought her some chocolate ice cream, and she cried in his arms as she opened up emotionally with him. Nick realized that she had been scared from past issues with her weight. He wanted to take away her pain. He had always loved her. In fact, she was his secret crush. He wanted to love her like no one had ever loved her before, but he knew that she was deeply distorted over Marcus. She may never love him back, because of this man's actions. So that night, he just held onto her as he knew best and tried to convince her that everything would be okay. When it started getting late, he left, but he assured her that he would be there to support him no matter what.

The next day, Anna woke up upset and wanting answers. She looked at her phone to see whether Marcus had called her. She had no missed calls from him. She decided to call him, nonetheless. Again, he picked up the phone and then hangs up before she could say anything. She kept calling repeatedly, until her calls started going directly to his voicemail, which was an indication that he had now switched off his phone.

Anna moped around the house for a little bit, but decided to take Nick's advise and took a shower and went job hunting. This time, she called the companies. Then, went there to fill out job applications. There was one company that was hiring. She was thrilled, and she got an interview with them the following morning. She called Nick to share the good news with him. It was a well-established accounting firm in Shreveport, which was a city about thirty minutes away from her hometown. Nick was elated for her, and he said that he would pray that she got the job.

On the morning of her interview, she was extremely nervous, but happy to find a company that was actually hiring people at the moment. She put on her best, most professional business suit and set out for the interview. When she got there, there was a long line of people, and she had to wait for about four hours before she could do her interview.

She kept her head high, went inside the interview room, and impressed the management team conducting the interview. She hadn't even arrived back home from the interview when she received the call from one of the managers informing her that she had been hired.

"Congratulations Miss Daniel! We enjoyed having you for the interview, and we would like to offer you the advertised position of Junior Auditor at our firm," he told her.

Had she not been driving, Anna would have jumped with joy. She thanked him over and over again, and immediately called her mom to give her the good news. Then, she called Nick to give him the good news as well. Both of them were really proud of her and were excited about her new job. Nick offered to take her and her mom out to dinner, to celebrate her new job.

Anna's first day at work was hectic. There were a lot of new concepts that she had to learn, but thankfully, she had always been a fast learner so it came easy for her. As the days and weeks went by, she became more settled into her job. Soon, she had made several friends at the office, and she was no longer the new girl. All the while, her relationship with Nick had blossomed into something beautiful. He was loving, understanding, kind, honest, respectful towards her, and she had to admit to herself that she had fallen in love with him. This was not a crush. It was a real genuine love.

Anna continued to allow her relationship with Nick to grow. She did not want to rush into anything.

It had been a little over a year now, since she had been back home. Nick's birthday was in a few days, and she had something very special planned for him. She booked a private massage for him at a spa owned by one of her mom's cousins.

Nick had taken the day of his birthday off from work, and Anna told him to meet her in the morning around nine. When he got to her house, his jaw dropped when he saw how stunning she looked. She had a silk pink dress, which accentuated her cleavage and her hourglass figure. She finished off her look with a pair of diamond earrings and a small diamond necklace. A stranger would have thought that it was her birthday, based on the way that she was dressed. "Happy Birthday, boo!" She shouted, and presented him with a small black gift bag. "You ready to go?" she said, as she walked out of her house.

"Thanks!" Nick replied, as he followed her. "So, where we going?" he continued.

"No, no, no, it's a surprise," she said placing her forefinger over his lips. "Now, give me your keys... I'm going to drive," she continued.

They drove for hours in the direction to Shreveport. When they arrived in Bossier City, she got off at one of the exits and drove off into a private road. They drove for about ten minutes until they stopped outside a building, which had "Vicki's Spa Central" written on the sign.

"Come on now, you have an appointment for ten," she said, as she hopped out looking at her watch. "Hurry baby, it's almost ten."

Nick had not been the type of guy who pampered or treated himself, although he would pamper and treat everybody else. When he got inside, there were three rooms and the doors were closed. There was a reception desk at her front with several waiting chairs. Anna went to speak with the reception. It seemed like they knew each other. The receptionist gave her the keys to one of the rooms. Anna took Nick by his hand and led him into one of the rooms. When they opened the door, there was a massage table and some massage oils in it.

"Happy birthday! I'll be your masseuse today," Anna told Nick with a smile on her face.

"Really," Nick replied. "Nah, I'm just kidding she said, "but I have something better for you," she said, as she left the room and another young lady came in. She was his masseuse. Nick never had a professional massage done before, and he really enjoyed it. When he walked out, Anna saw that he was more relaxed, and she was happy that she had arranged this new experience for him. She then drove him over to a nearby hotel, where she had reserved a room for the two of them.

He opened the door and walked into the room. The first thing he saw as the amazing view of Bossier City from the glass doors in the room. Then he looked to the side of the bed, and there was a huge Jacuzzi that could easily accommodate about six or eight people in it all at the same time. As his eyes continued to cruise through the room, he saw a plate with some strawberries and chocolate syrup on it, and a bottle of red wine with two wine glasses next to the plate.

They entered the room, and he sat on the bed. Anna walked over to the radio and turned on some music. He was impressed with her. She had really gone all out for his birthday. She then walked over to the Jacuzzi, filled it with water, and put a little bubble bath soap into the water. She then walked over to him, held his hand and led him over to the Jacuzzi.

"You know, I'm really feeling you," he told her. She nodded her head and replied,

"This was why I arranged all of this, 'cause I'm really feeling you, too."

They both smiled when they heard that the feeling was mutual. They had always been open and honest about everything, but it seemed like they were both shy and could not muster up the courage to admit their true feelings. He took her hands into his. He had been waiting for a moment like this with her, for a while now.

He slowly leaned closer to her and gently implanted a soft kiss upon her lips. She smelled so sweet, like she had just gotten out of the shower. He wanted to do so much more to her, but he held back. She unzipped her dress and was wearing a matching red, lace bra and thong. He could see her sexy naked body now, and her skin looked like sweet dark chocolate. He was definitely attracted to her. He, too, removed his clothes and stood there wearing only his boxers.

She went into the Jacuzzi first, and he followed suit. They each sat at one end of the Jacuzzi, looking directly at each other.

"Let me just slide over here," he said, as he moved in closer to her. She smiled, got up, and sat directly behind him. "Relax baby! Let me wash this massage oil off," she said, as she took a washcloth and gently passed it all over his body.

He enjoyed the body scrub, but he wanted her bad, and his dick was throbbing in the water.

He swiftly turned around. He was now directly in front of her. He kissed her soft lips, and they both feel the passion in the kiss. This was long overdue, and they knew it. Their passion got a hold of them, and they were kissing each other and moaning right there, in the Jacuzzi. He reached behind her and removed her bra. Her breast were full and bouncy. He could not resist putting his lips on her nipples. He licked and sucked them gently, as his hands roamed under the water.

Finally, they found their destination, her pussy. She moaned as he slips his hands inside her panties. He could feel her clitoris, and it felt tiny. He then glided his finger further down her, and soon it reached the pussy hole. He gently stroked it, as their kissing got more intense. She moaned with pleasure, and he loved it.

Although she was enjoying herself in the Jacuzzi, she had other plans. So, she gradually pulled away from his grasp and got up out of the Jacuzzi. "Come, let's got out of this Jacuzzi," she told him. He was too weak with desire to go against anything she said. He was like her slave, and she was his master. They headed over to the bed, and she told him to lie down on the bed, on his back. Then, she climbed on top of him and proceeded to pick up where they left off. They were kissing even more passionately now. As he kissed her, he rips off her thong and flings it across the room. She was now completely naked and began rubbing her pussy against his skin. He went wild when he felt her wet pussy.

"You're so wet," he said to her.

"Yeah," she replied. "I had been looking forward to this day for some time now." She continued with a smile on her face. He kissed her, as to indicate that he, too, had wanted her for a while now. As they kissed each other, the intensity of their desires became almost unbearable, and she got to the point where she wanted to suck his dick. She slowly traced downwards on his body, from his neck to his groin. She removed his boxers and his dick was exposed. He saw the look of surprise in her eyes when she saw his dick. She would had never thought that he had such a big dick. His dick was long and thick. It was a dark brown complexion and it was straight, without any curves. However, there were about three big, long, dark veins running along it. She immediately put her lips on the head of the dick, and then gradually tried to suck the entire thing. It was so big that she gagged when she tried to put his entire dick in her mouth. His body tensed up, as he felt an electrifying sensation from her tongue on his dick.

"Oh Anna," he groaned, as she began working her tongue all over his dick. Her tongue was hot and wet, and she was ravishing his dick with it. She sucked it long and hard. Then, she increased her pace and her sucks were faster and harder. She used her tongue to explore the sides of the head of his dick. He almost went crazy. "Where did you learn to do all that?" he had to ask her.

"I watch porn, too, you know," she said with a wicked smile on her face. She reached over and gently cupped his balls and begun to slowly fondle and caress them while sucking his dick. "Oh God, Anna... Anna..." he groaned. It was like she knew his body. Every touch... Every lick... Every suck caused tiny spasms to jolt through his body. His dick almost doubled in size as she sucked on it. She had never experienced this.

Anna reached over into the nightstand draw, and pulled out a Trojan bare skin condom that she had placed there. She unwrapped the condom and tried to put it on his dick as best as she could. As soon as it was all the way on, she climbed on top of his dick and gently glided her pussy down his pleasure stick. When his dick was inside her wet pussy, she began riding it back and forth, up and down. Nick held onto her butt cheeks as he slammed his dick upwards inside her pussy. She moaned with every thrust, and she could feel his dick throbbing while he was fucking her. He was groaning as he ravished her insides with his monster cock.

"Oh yes," she moaned, as she bounced back and forth on his dick.

"Yeah," he said, as he increased the intensity of his thrusts. They were both in ecstasy, and they could almost feel each other's heartbeat. "I love you," he groaned, as he thrust even harder into her.

When she heard that, she began kissing him while riding his dick. She kissed him long and hard. She pulled back, and told him that she loved him too. In the heat of the moment, they had finally confessed their love for each other. She continued riding his dick. They both climaxed together.

It was amazing, and it took a while for their bodies to calm down and return to reality.

When they were relaxed, she went over and got the strawberries and chocolate syrup. They sat on the floor and feed each other, while sipping on some red wine.

"I do really love you," he said to her.

"I know you do baby, and I love you too." Finally, they were comfortable enough with each other to confess their love. It had not been an hour from when they last made love, but they were filled with an intense desire for each other once more. They made love again, right there on the floor. This time was even more earth shattering than their first time. She had finally found love, but it was not with her secret crush. It was with her best friend.

4 THE BATTLE WITHIN HIM

As Chad walked into the lobby of the Jewel Hotel, he could feel the stares of the people around penetrating through his skin. This was his first day on the job at the hotel, in the position of IT manager, and he was so nervous he could feel his knees shaking. He took the small, narrow stairs in the back, and went up to the administration office. He opened the door and, low and behold, there were about eight women looking at him, from his head to his feet.

"Good morning," he said. "I'm Chad, the new IT manager," he continued, as he closed the door behind him and made his way through the small group of women. Chad Harrison was a strikingly handsome young man, with a rich brown chocolate complexion and dark, wavy, neatly cut hair. He had a lean, athletic body and, to top it off, he had the most gorgeous smile with a set of pearly white teeth. He was the envy of most men around town. He was well-known for his good looks, and his player type attitude.

It came as no surprise to him that he was hired in a managerial position, although he had no managerial or hospitality experience. Ms. Jackson, who was the hotel manager that interviewed him, barely looked at his resume. He knew that his good looks would be all that he needed to persuade her into hiring him.

Chad got to the door of the general manager's office and, after knocking about two times, he heard her voice asking him to come in. She welcomed him to the company.

Then, she handed him his employment contract, which he had to date and sign at the bottom, after reading all the terms of his employment and job description. "Ok wonderful. Now that's done. I'll have Monica, my admin assistant, take you around to the different departments to introduce you and just, basically, show you the systems that we use here," she said, as she picked up the phone to call Monica.

Chad could swear that Ms. Jackson had not even ended the call with her assistant when they heard the knock on the door. He heard a soft, feminine voice at the other end saying, "Can I come in?" Chad was a little anxious to see the person behind the door with this cool, calm tone of voice.

The door opened slowly, and Chad saw an attractive young woman of African American decent, like him, walk in.

"Hi, I'm Monica." She said, as she extended her tiny hands out to him, requesting a handshake. She was a slender, young woman who looked like she was just out of college.

She had her silky black hair all back in a ponytail, and wore a figure hugging work dress with a cute pair of pencil heels. As he extended his hand to hers, he felt her soft, warm, tender grasp, and he longed to get to know this woman better.

They soon headed out the door for the tour of the hotel, as she introduced him to the other employees. He could see that they all had warm, positive attitudes toward her. He desperately wanted to find out more about her, and possibly take her out on a few dates, but he did not know how to ask her. He had been told of the hotel's strict policy against managers and line staff having personal relationships.

As they sat down for lunch at midday, he decided that now would be the perfect opportunity to find out about her. The more they talked, the more he became interested in getting to know her better. Although the urge was there for him to ask her out on a date, he decided to keep their relationship strictly professional.

It had been almost six months since Chad started his new job, and it had been going great. He was working in an environment with only women, and they were extra nice to him. They would always bring him little treats, and offer to help him out with his daily reports and other tasks around the office that he had to do.

However, Monica was different from the other women. Although she was pleasant to him, she kept to herself most of the time. It almost seemed like she had been avoiding him.

As Friday approached, he looked forward to going to the bar, possibly picking up some chick there, and having a one-night stand with her, like he normally did when he got paid. Every time he went to the bar, he went there with every intention of meeting someone and ending their evening back at his apartment, after a night of hot sex.

Soon enough, it was Friday evening. As he walked into the bar, he immediately began scanning his environment, looking for the attractive woman that he could entice with his charm.

Surprisingly, his eyes caught wind of a familiar face at the table in the right corner of the bar. It was none other than Monica, his co-worker. He looked at her from a distance, trying to figure out what his next move would be.

She looked angelic. Her hair was not in a ponytail, like how she normally wore it at work. It was loose, and ran down her shoulders. She looked rather lonely. Finally, he stood up and walked over to where she was seated.

"Wow, didn't think that I'd see you here," he said, as he got next to her.

"Hey," she replied, with a smile on her face.

He pulled out a chair and sat next to her. The loud music made it almost impossible to hear her from across the table. "So, what were you doing here? Thought you'd be at home," he said to her. "Well, I just been so busy at work and stuff, I figured I could treat myself to a few drinks." She replied. They drank straight shots the entire time and engaged in a very lively conversation, sharing jokes and funny experiences with each other. They definitely had real chemistry between them.

They decided to go back to her apartment to chat some more, once they were tired of being at the bar.

Monica had a beautiful, neatly organized studio apartment in the city, in one of the luxury apartment buildings. The view from her small patio was spectacular. Chad could see the ocean and all the Miami city lights.

She came to join him on the patio with a bottle of red wine, and two wine glasses. They savored the moment, as they sipped on their red wine. This was the opportune time for him to express his feelings toward her. He swept in and gently planted a wet kiss on her soft, pink lips.

She welcomed his kisses with parted lips and their tongues went wild with passion. Chad's dick leaped with joy as he felt her tongue ravishing his tongue. A signal, that she, too, wanted him. He groped onto both of her butt cheeks and pulled her in closer to him. He could feel tiny spasms running through his body.

In the heat of the moment, he lifted her up and places her on the small, round table right there on the patio. As they continued to kiss, Chad used his fingers to undo the buttons of her blouse.

He now exposed the sexy, black lace bra that she was wearing. Her breasts were so tempting and he could not resist the urge to release them from the bra. As he removed the bra, and flung it to the other side of the patio, her full breasts bounced out of place. Her breasts were perfectly shaped and he could tell that she doesn't have any children as of yet, from their firmness. As he grabbed hold of her nipple with his mouth, she moaned out loud. "Oh, yeah," she said, as she tilted her head backwards and pushed her chest outwards.

He held one breast and focuses his attention on each breast one by one, licking, sucking, and occasionally, gently biting the nipples. Chad jolted back a little when he felt her tight grip on his hard dick. He had not even noticed that she unzipped his pants, and had found his huge manhood. As he caresses her nipples, she gently, in turn, strokes his dick. Her grip tightens, as she increases the momentum of the hand job that she was giving him. Chad had had enough and pulled away from her grasp, only to have her lie down on the table and spread her legs apart.

"I had wanted you from the first time I saw you," he confessed to her, as he gently works his way into her inner thighs with his tongue.

"Reallllyyyyyyyyyyyyy," she said moaning.

"Yes," he replied, as he reached her clean, shaved pussy. Chad wanted her so bad that he was now terrified that he would explode before getting the opportunity to feel her inner flesh on his dick. He put his tongue on her pink pussy lips, and gives it a good slow lick. Up and down, up and down. He licked her pussy with his tongue. She was trying to grab onto the sides of the table for support, as the pleasure that he was giving to her seems too intense for her to bear.

"Aww, yeah, ummm... Yeah, Oh," she moaned. "Oh yes." In a faster tone, "Oh yes, yes, yes," she moaned in a rapid tone of voice as her legs twitch and turn, as he sucked the life out of her pussy. When he realized that she was about to cum, he pulled away quickly, "I want you to cum on my dick ok," he said. "You're gonna have to hold back for now. I want to feel your cum all over my dick," he continued, as he gave her a wicked smile. She could hardly respond. She simply nodded her head in agreement.

Chad removed his pants and his dick popped out, showing its full length. His dick was brown, with small veins running across it from the top to the bottom. When she saw his dick, he saw her eyes light up with approval, and he knew that she was impressed. He stroked his dick a few times with his hands, as if preparing his dick before plunging it inside her. As he thrust his huge dick inside her, she closed her eyes. It seemed like she was concentrating on how to get her pussy to open up wider, to accommodate his huge cock.

"Awwwwwwwwwwwww," he groaned, as he went deeper and deeper inside her pussy with his dick. Finally, his dick was inside her pussy, and he gradually pulled it back out, only to stick it in again. This time, it was even harder, faster, than before.

"O SHIT! God DAMN!" She shrieked, as he began to use his dick like a dagger, stabbing her pussy with his weapon over and over again. The table that she was laying on was rocking violently back and forth, back and forth. Her moans could be heard as Chad was thrusting inside her tiny pussy with his huge dick. He looked down at her face, and he could see her facial expressions changing with every thrust. She had her eyes closed. She occasionally licked her lips, and took deep breaths. Chad decided to slow it down a little. He began talking dirty to her, to increase their pleasure.

"You like this dick, don't you," he said, as he gave her a hard thrust.

"Uh huh," she replied, licking her lips.

"No, you're gonna had to answer me, Monica," he said, in a disapproving tone of voice. "You like this dick? Yes or NO?" he said, as he thrust his dick even deeper and harder inside her pussy.

"Yes, Yes!" She exclaimed. "Good girl," he replied, now with a smile on his face, as he got a little gentle with his strokes, giving her long, slow strokes. She was so slender that he could see the movement of his dick inside her with every thrust. He continued to penetrate her with his dick, until he felt like he was about to explode inside her. "Oh God! I'm going to cum," he said, as he pulled his dick outside of her, as quickly as he could. His ejaculation shot all over her stomach. He used his hands to ensure that all of his hot liquid was all over her. As he watched her body on the table, he could tell that she had not climaxed and she was still very horny. Without thinking twice, he immediately went down on her and pleasured her with his tongue. His tongue drove her crazy. Her body twisted and turned in every direction, as her knees trembled from the ecstasy.

"O, my, my, uhhhhhhhhhhhhhh," she moaned out loud. "Yes, Yes, Yes, Yes," she said, in a voice that was like a song that kept getting louder. "OO, YES!" she finally exclaimed, as she reached her climax and exploded with cum.

He had to give her a few minutes to calm down and collect herself. "Wow, you definitely had a good cum," he said to her, with a smile on his face. She looked at him and giggled like she was an embarrassed child. He sensed that she was probably embarrassed. So, he decided to assure her that he was actually impressed by the way she was able to enjoy their erotic encounter on the patio. "I like the way you came, don't be shy. I like a woman who could get a climax and really enjoy it," he said to her, as he kissed her on her forehead. After a while, she got up off the table and they proceeded to go inside the room. He made sure that she was in bed, before calling a cab to take him home.

The weekend was going good for Chad, and he felt as though he needed to call Monica. Just to make sure that they were cool. He looked in his phone to find her number, but realized that they had never exchanged numbers. He was so upset with himself. How could he have been so attracted to this woman, yet, know so little about her? "Well, I'll just have to get her number on Monday," he thought to himself. As the day progressed, it was almost unbearable. He needed to speak to her, or even see her. It was Saturday evening when he decided that he needed to go find her. He tried to retrace their steps the previous night, in an effort to remember her address. It was one of the luxury condo building on the waterfront, but there were about six of them, and he did not know which one. As he got to the beach, he decided to stand in front of each building to see which one had the view of the ocean, like her room. He soon discovered that she lived in the second building. He went to the front door of the building and told the lobby attendant that he was there to see Monica.

"You would like to see Monica who? What apartment are you going to?" The lobby attendant asked, with a concerned look on her face. She was a short, angry looking, chubby woman.

"Well, I'm her co-worker. She works at the Jewel Hotel. If you call her apartment, she'll know who I am and say it's ok," he tried to reassure the attendant.

"You best believe I'm gonna call her mister," she said, as she picked up the phone on her desk and dialed a number. "Hi, Miss Monica, there's a gentleman here to see you. He said he works at the hotel with you, but he didn't even know your name or apartment," she said to the person on the other end of the phone. He looked at her with his fingers crossed, hoping that there was only one Monica at this building, and that Monica would let him come up to see her.

"Ok, Miss Monica," she said, as she ended the call. "You can go up to see her. Its Apartment 3E on the ninth floor," she said to Chad. He hopped into the elevator and anxiously waited for it to stop at his destination.

Monica opened the door and let him in, by the second knock. "Hey," she said, as she invited him in with her hands.

"Hey, yourself," he said as he walked in. "I just stopped by to make sure we were straight. You know, like, I don't want what happened in the heat of the moment last night to come between us," he informed her.

"Well, I'm cool," she said smiling. "We both had a little too much to drink, and it just sorta happened, but it's not going to affect our work relationship," she continued.

"Yeah, definitely," he said, as he moved in closer to her, like she was being attracted to a magnet. She was wearing a loose, white blouse with buttons at the front, a few inches above her knee. It did not appear that she was wearing any pants with it. He had a hard on from the time he saw her strikingly long, sexy legs. This woman had an effect that few people ever had on him, but he needed to stop himself before it was too late.

"Well, just came by, 'cause I wanted to make sure everything was cool between us," he said, as his eyes looked directly at hers.

He tried to walk away, but just when he was about to leave, and she was closing the door, he had the strong desire to kiss her. Like two people possessed, they instantly began kissing each other. He made his way back into her room, and closed the door behind him. He pushed her up against the wall of the apartment, and they kissed each other more passionately than they had done the night before. This time, he yanked her legs up, pulled out his dick, and begun fucking her, right there on the wall. She moaned with pleasure, as he thrust his dick upwards inside her pussy. He began ripping off her clothes. They were like two savage animals ravishing each other's bodies.

"Oh baby, yeah, just like... Don't stop... Oooo," she moaned, as he continued to bang his dick upwards inside her pussy, causing her body to bounce up and down against the wall. Their desires for each other had multiplied by one hundred. As they made love on the wall, their bodies craved more and more.

"Oh Monica," Chad groaned, as the two of them gave into their desires and they climaxed together. They could hardly believe what had just happened, afterwards.

"So darn, we did it again," he said smiling. She too smiled, as they stood there with their clothes spread all over the floor. Her pussy was dripping with his cum. She excused herself and went to the washroom. When she came out, she invited him to stay over for dinner. They enjoyed dinner and for desert, they enjoyed each other's caressing, making love to each other. Before leaving that night, Chad ensured that he had her number, and promised to call her as soon as he got home.

The weekend had gone great for Chad. As he walked into the office, he noticed something different about Monica. She was giving him the evil eye. It was then that he remembered that he had promised to call her on Saturday night, but he never did. In fact, he did not call her on Sunday, either. How could this had happened. Sure, Saturday night, when he got home he was so exhausted that he went straight to bed, but Sunday, he should have made it his duty to call her. He walked up to her desk and asked if he could see her in private. She barely looked at him, and told him that she was busy and did not think it was a good idea that they speak, period. He decided to apologize to her, right there.

"I am soo, soo, soo sorry for not calling you. It just completely slipped my mind," he said to her, hoping that she would understand and give him a positive response.

"Really, it slipped your mind, huh? Funny, how my address did not slip your mind on Saturday. You sure found me, but I understand. I made it too easy for you. So, I got it! You hit it and quit it, but don't come back now. Don't talk to me, 'cause what happened between us will never, NEVER, EVER, happen again," she said in a firm tone of voice.

He could tell that she was hurt, and he could see that she needed her space. So, he walked away from her.

He almost fainted when he heard his manager's voice saying, "What happened over the weekend Chad? What's going on between you and Monica?" she said, as she looked at him directly in his eye, as if she were trying to extract the truth out of him.

"Um, nothing." He said. As he tried to quickly brush her off and evade any more of her questions.

"No Chad, we need to talk now. My office," she said in an authoritative tone of voice.

When Chad entered the office, he was even more shocked to hear the next set of words that came out of her mouth. "You're a very attractive young man, Chad, and I know I definitely did not hire you to sleep with my assistant. If you want someone like her, you could have me," she said, as she came closer to him, in a seductive way.

Chad knew that she was attracted to him, based on the way she would look at him. Even from his interview, the way she didn't even ask about references, or anything job related, but he was taken aback by her straightforward attempt at getting with him.

"I will not tolerate you having relations with any other female in this hotel, you hear me

Chad?" she said, as she came closer to him. She pushed him backwards, causing him to fall onto a small sofa that she had in her office.

Chad was astonished and could barely say anything. It was such a viciously fierce attack. Women had constantly been throwing themselves at him, and he had enjoyed the benefits of his good looks in the past. But, here he was with this much older woman, who was his manager, and now, apparently trying to blackmail him into having sex with her.

"Chad, you will have to choose between your job and Monica, you know. If you were seeing her? I won't have you working here, with your fine self, and sleeping with that girl. If anybody's gonna be getting a piece of this dark chocolate, it's gonna be me," she said, as she passed her tongue along the right side of his face.

Chad did not know what to do. This was the best job that he had from the time he left college, but he did not want to sleep with this woman. Although he and Monica had only recently become psychical, the truth was, he always had a crush on her from the first day he met her. Chad felt like he was fighting a losing battle, because he would have to sacrifice this hot new passion that he discovered for his job.

As his mind went into wondering mode, Ms. Jackson continued her advances on him and stripped him of his clothes. She climbed on top of him, as he sat on the couch. He tried to convince her that what they were doing was wrong, and he did not want any relations with

Monica, but she was a determined woman with a mission. He felt violated in every way, while she used her hands and explored his private parts.

She went down on him, while he sat on the chair, and sucked his dick. All the while, he was trying to convince her to stop. When she got up, and put her wet pussy on his semi-hard dick, he gave in. She took control of his body and rode his dick, bouncing up and down on it with her pussy. She was getting so much pleasure from it, he was in shock. When he was about to ejaculate, he pulled her off his dick and stroked his dick with his hands, as his semen shot out in every direction.

"That was amazing," she said, as she put on her outfit. "Now, clean your mess and got dressed. I have a meeting in here in the next ten minutes," she ordered. Chad had never felt so used in his life. Now, he knew how the women he had the one night stands with must have felt, and even how Monica must have felt, after he did not call her after making such a huge effort to see her.

As he walked out of the room, he felt embarrassed as the women looked at him with a look of suspicion on their faces. More importantly, he looked at Monica in the corner, where she sat. He could see a small line of tears running down her face. The women had all heard what had taken place in the office. The moans, the groans, even the squeaking of the springs in the couch where they had been fucking.

Chad was so disappointed and disgusted with himself. He walked out of the office without even looking back. The hotel was a small property, and soon the gossip spread like wildfire. Each day Chad would come to work hoping that this would be the day when Monica would speak to him, but it never was. In fact, every other day, Ms. Jackson made it a habit to have him in her office, and she just always had her way with him. Sometimes she would just suck his dick. Other times, she would order him to suck her pussy. Sometimes they would fuck. After a few months, Chad became known around the hotel as Ms. Jackson's male whore. A few of his male co-workers would even throw words at him. It was a very uncomfortable, disgusting situation for him. The entire time, Chad was missing Monica terribly. He would often sit at his desk just looking at her. Wondering what he had missed out on. This could had possibly been his future wife, but now, he would never know, because she could not even look him in the eye.

After months of what seemed like torture, Chad walked up to Monica's desk, once more and apologized this time. He could not hide his feelings towards her. As time had passed, he had fallen in love with her, and he would do just about anything to have her in his life. He hated the way they never got the opportunity to really explore a relationship together. He also hated the way he hurt her.

As he stood in front of her desk apologizing, profusely, the other women in the office came around them, with curious eyes, listening in on his conversation with her. Soon enough, everyone spread out, and he heard a voice that he had begun to loathe over the months. "What's going on here?" Ms. Jackson asked in a firm voice. "Chad. Are you crying?" she continued, with a weird look of surprise on her face.

Chad had enough; he finally looked up at her. For the first time, he told her what was on his mind. "Don't ask me what's wrong... you did this to me. I actually liked this woman, but because of you and your selfish desires, she won't even look at me. I don't want to be with you, Ms. Jackson. You need to understand that. This was who I want!" he said, as he pointed to Monica.

"I am sorry; I don't want to be with you. I'm sorry, and it's frustrating that you keep threatening to take away my job if I don't let you use me and my body. But, it stops today, 'cause I... I love this woman, man," he said, as he broke down into tears. "And... I wish she would listen to me, and hear the sincerity in my voice."

He went down on his knees in front of Monica's desk. "Monica, baby, I'm talking from the heart. You had me attracted to you from day one, when I saw you. Yeah, I've been around. I've been with a couple of women, but none of them got me like you do. I mean, we not even together, but I love you from the bottom of my heart, girl," he continued.

Monica's eyes filled with tears, as she

slowly looked at him. She looked directly into his eyes, trying to find his soul. His tears were sincere and, as he was down on his knees. She kept having flashbacks of the few moments of passion that they had shared in the past.

"WELL, you want to be like that, you ungrateful bastard," Ms. Jackson exclaimed, "You're FIRED!! Yeah, both you and your little slutty girlfriend! Get the FUCK out of my hotel!" She shrieked, as she also burst into tears. It appears that she, in turn, in some strange kind of way, had fallen in love with Chad, and was very hurt by his words and actions.

"Well, Ms. Jackson, that's fine by me," Chad said, as he got up off his knees and began walking away. "You coming baby?" he turned around and said to Monica, who had already started clearing out her drawers.

"Yeah," she sprung up out of her seat, and left the stuff that she had been packing, taking only her small, black work bag with her. The two of them left the office and headed straight back to Monica's apartment.

When they arrived at the apartment, they barely made it inside before they started passionately kissing each other. As they kissed each other, they were both apologizing to each other for their behavior. They were both so desperately seeking to be with each other that they almost made love on the floor of the apartment. Chad tried to control his body, and did not want to rush through this experience with her. He had been waiting too long to do this again with her. He gently undressed her, and laid her down on her bed. She looked so beautiful. Her body was glowing and he instantly began to make love to her body, inch by inch.

He took her big toe into his mouth and sucked it. She moaned, as she enjoyed this sensation that she had never before felt in her life. He worked his way up her legs, using his wicked tongue to drive her wild. When he got to her pussy, he ravished her with his hot wet tongue, sucking her pussy like she had never been sucked before.

She moaned with pleasure, and her moans were loud and almost in a different language. He used his tongue to explore the insides of her pussy, having her gripping onto the sheets and gasping for air.

The more he licked and sucked her pussy, the more she moaned. Her moaned became a sweet song to his ear, "Ohh babbyyyyyyyyyy... Oh yesssssssssssssss... Chaddddddddddddd..." she moaned, as he used his tongue to sweep through her pink pussy lips. He then focused on getting her to orgasm by sucking onto her clitoris.

He licked it and then sucked it, while using his index finger to finger fuck her wet pussy. "Oh shit... Yeahhhhhhhh... Yeahhhh... Yeahhhhhhhhhhh... Baby... Chad, yeah oooo! Oh GOD... YES! YES! YES!" She exclaimed with pleasure, as she came all over his tongue.

"Baby, you taste soo good," he said, as he licked all of her cum as if he were licking some sweet juice dripping from her pussy.

He then pulled out his hard, long cock, and thrusts it inside her pussy. Chad held her legs up in the air, allowing him full access inside her pussy, maximizing his penetration strokes.

"UH!" He groaned, as he shoves his dick deep inside her. "UH.. UH.. UH!" He continued groaning, as he penetrated her pussy over and over with his large, long cock. Monica moaned with pleasure, and grabbed his butt cheeks, as if to help assist him with his thrust.

Chad continued thrusting his dick inside her pussy with long, hard strokes. Then, he increases his momentum, causing her to moan and cries like a baby. "O yeahhhh, uhhh, uhh," she moaned, as he fucked her soo hard that her body quivered every time he slammed his cock inside her pussy. "Oh SHIT... Yeah... Baby... Am... Cuming... O... YEA... YESSSSSSS... UHHHHHHHHHHHH!!!!!!!!!!!!!" He groaned loudly, as he exploded inside her. They both climaxed together. Their bodies shook viciously, from the intensity of their experience and they both lay down on the bed next to each other.

"I love you, Monica," he said, "... and I don't want any of these other women. I just want you, no one else."

Monica looked at him. She knew that his words were coming from a place deep down within him. It was not only coming from his heart, it was coming from his soul. In all her life, she had never seen a man cry out to her before. Yet, Chad had done it at work, in front of everyone. She knew that he had to be sincere. "I love you too, Chad, with all my heart."

She replied, as she put her head on his shoulders. Chad kissed her on her forehead, as he smiled a smile of victory. With her by his side, he knew that he would not want anybody else. He won the battle that he had been fighting all his life. He would be faithful to her. He never wanted to hurt her the way that he hurt her before. He loved this woman with every fiber in his bone.

5 THE COUGAR KILLER

She waited until all the lights were out and everyone was asleep. As Denise picked up her phone, she went to the corner of her room and dialled the number of her most recent missed call. Speaking in a very low tone of voice, she informed the person on the other end of the call that she was ready. Her heart raced as she snuck out of her half opened bedroom window. The fear that she might get caught almost made her change her mind. In less than ten minutes, a gray car pulled up a short distance from her house and the driver blinked the lights three times.

This was her signal. She swiftly made her way through her mom's flower garden looking back at the house a couple of times to ensure that no one had seen her. As she got in the car she was greeted by the handsome Jonathan Taylor. He was by far the most attractive guy at Hunter State University. He was also the most popular guy. As captain of the football team, the girls practically threw themselves at him. Denise blushed as he spoke to her, trying hard to conceal her nervousness; it was a privilege to be out on a date with him. When people saw them together at this party, she would definitely score some cool points and maybe even change her nerdy image.

They pulled up to a secluded mansion a good distance from the highway. This would be her first college frat party, and she did not know what would happen or who would be there. As they opened the front door she pulled down her black spandex mini dress, wishing that she had worn some jeans instead. The music was deafening and the place was lit up with tiny globes of red and yellow lights hanging from the ceiling. There were so many people that it was difficult to make their way inside.

"Don't worry, I'll take care of you," Jonathan said to her, when he realized the dazed look on her face. He led her to the kitchen area where he introduced her to three of his friends. She recognized them; they were all athletes like him. He poured her a glass of what seemed like punch. She almost puked when she took her first gulp of this very alcoholic drink which seemed more like whiskey.

Denise wanted to throw away the rest of the drink, but she could see the guys watching her with curious eyes, as if waiting for her to be done with the drink. Taking a silent deep breath she thought to herself, 'this was easy, I could do this,' and swallowed the rest of the drink.

The drinks kept coming as the night went on, and it got to the point to where Denise did not really feel the burning sensation that the drink had first left behind as it trickled down the back of her throat.

She was now feeling overly excited, yet relaxed - very relaxed. She swerved around a little tilting her head back, as she watched the ceiling spin around. She felt like she was the center of the universe and nothing else or no one else mattered at that moment. She laughed loud as she staggered around the house, with a drink in her hand. She was in such a mellow mood that she did not even resist the hand that had grabbed her arm, and was now leading her upstairs. The next thing she knew, she was lying down on her back on a big, soft bed. As she looked at the ceiling, her eyes caught a familiar face. It was Jonathan. He was on top of her, and she was now feeling his strong, masculine hands making their way up her dress. She was enjoying the feelings that his touch brought about when she heard another voice in the room.

"Hurry up man, we all want a go at her," he said, with desperation and longing in his voice. What was going on here? she thought to herself as she tried to sit up to see where the strange new voice came from.

Her eyes caught sight of the three other masculine figures in the room. Although she was somewhat out of it, she was still half conscious, and knew what they were trying to do.

"No, Jonathan, I'm not down for this," she said as she tried to sit up and leave the room. The shove took her by surprise and she was about to scream, when he used his hands to firmly squeeze her tiny neck. "Now listen, bitch, we could do this the easy way, or the hard way. Either way, no one is gonna hear you!" Jonathan roared at her as his face changed from cool and calm to wicked and harsh. Denise tried to fight back, but she realized that she was too intoxicated to actually stop what was about to happen.

He pulled her tiny dress off her and tossed it into a corner of the room. She had not been wearing a bra, and so her tiny round breasts were exposed, much to his delight. His eyes carefully examined her petite, perfectly-shaped, chocolate brown body. He ripped away her panties and also threw it away to the side of the bed. She looked at him, staring directly into his hazel eyes; they were lit up with desire.

He now used his hands to stroke her inner thighs, and when he got to her clit, he rubbed on it. At first his finger action was slow and sensual, but then as his visible erection increased, he became rougher and rougher with her. "You a virgin?" he asked her with curious eyes.

She took a while to answer him, as if trying to hide the fact. "Well, you know, I'm gonna find out." he said to her as a devious smile formed at the corners of his mouth. He continued to use his index finger to probe the insides of her pussy.

Although at first she was in opposition to this she was now beginning to really enjoy the way he was pleasuring her. She moaned with the sound of pleasure and approval in her voice. Suddenly, as she lay on the bed, her view of the ceiling was blocked off by a massive black cock dangling in front her.

"Suck it bitch, c'mon," the voice behind the dick instructed her. In the heat of the moment, she instantly opened her mouth and welcomed his raw meat. The guy was enjoying this and moved around a little before he found a comfortable position, while he plunged his huge dick inside her mouth. She sucked the long hard dick, as hard as she could, which in turn caused him to groan loud and even swear a few times.

Denise's attention on the blowjob that she was giving was cut short due the immense pressure she felt between her legs. Jonathan was penetrating her tiny pussy with his huge, black dick. She felt every inch of his long dick as it forced its way inside her core. He could tell that she was not a virgin, but yet, her pussy was so tight, he knew that she was probably inactive down there. Her body cringed as his dick continued its upward thrust inside of her, and the only reason she did not scream out for dear God, was because of the huge dick stuffed in her mouth.

Jonathan continued to thrust his dick inside her pussy several times, each time harder and deeper than the next. As he fucked her, his sweat fell on her body as he gripped onto her waist area with both his hands, one on each side.

"My turn, I need to get in there," a horny voice said from a corner of the room. The alcohol in her system caused Denise to have very little control of her body or who accessed her holes. Jonathan pulled away from her, and some other guy managed to fit himself between her and Jonathan.

She pulled her lips off of the guy's dick and shrieked in pain when she felt this new stranger forcing his dick up against her anus. He used his salvia as lubrication and fingered her ass a little before penetrating it with his dick. As his dick went upwards inside her ass, she gripped onto the sheets and clenched her teeth. The pain was intense and although she was drunk, she could tell the difference between pleasure and pain.

She moaned out begging him to stop, but her pleas fell on deaf ears. These guys were too engrossed in their desire to fuck her to hear anything that she had to say.

The penetrations began once more, a dick in the mouth, a dick in the pussy and a dick in the ass. The three dicks simultaneously thrust in and out of her three holes, while the guys groaned and groaned, licking their lips occasionally giving each other hi-fives. They were exactly the type of guys her mom used to warn her about, the horny college guys that would do anything to fuck other people's daughters. As they used her limp body, she could not do anything. She moaned and moaned as they fucked the life out of her. After a while the unbearable pain totally transformed to unbearable pleasure, and Denise now found herself coming alive to their every stroke. As Jonathan thrusts his big dick in and out of her pussy, she could feel tiny sensations running through her body.

Just as she indulged in the sensations that she felt in her pussy, she felt the immense pleasure of the dick that was being thrust viciously in her ass. That was something she had never done before, because of the initial pain of the penetration. However, anal sex for her was now becoming an amazing experience. She expressed her pleasure by sucking onto the dick in her mouth with more desire. The way she moved her tongue all over his dick and flicked it back and forth on the head, had the guy in sweet heaven. His groans were filled with desire, and he was the first out of the three to lose control.

The sudden taste of hot liquid in her mouth caused her to pull her lips away from his dick. As she tried not to concentrate too much on its awful taste, her mouth was stuffed with dick again. But this dick tasted different. She looked up and her eyes caught Jonathan's desire inflamed eyes. He shoved his dick violently in her mouth. She did not mind. She sucked on it, giving it fast hard strokes with her tongue. Over and over, she pleasured his dick with her tongue, until he too exploded his ocean of semen inside of her mouth. He groaned with a sigh of relief when he ejaculated. She watched as he stepped away from her.

As she was about to sit up, she felt a strong macular hand firmly push her body back on the bed. Before she could resist the third dick was shoved into her exhausted mouth.

"C'mon, suck my dick too, baby," he said as if begging her to release him of this juices. Feeling like she did not have a choice, she licked the erect dick. Her mouth went back and forth on it, and the guy was enjoying it so much that he was now using his thumb and index finger to caress her nipples. Denise moaned out with pure ecstasy in her voice.

"Look at the little slut enjoy Trey's dick," she heard one of them say as she continued to suck his dick. Soon enough the momentum of the thrusts in her mouth increased and with a loud outstretched groan, this third guy exploded into her mouth.

The three men put on their clothes, and when they were leaving the room, Jonathan threw her clothes at her.

"Get dressed; I'm taking you home in a minute." Denise put on her clothes, and the realization of what had just happened set in. These three guys had completely violated her, and although she enjoyed it, at first she had resisted. How would she ever show her face at school again? After some time Jonathan came back to the room to get her, and he took her home like he had said he would.

The ride home was a quiet one, and as she looked at him, he no longer looked like the handsome guy he had seemed to be earlier in the evening when he had picked her up. He was mean and wicked. In fact, he was gross, and disgusting, and she suddenly felt a churning in her stomach and leaned forward a little.

"What the fuck!" Jonathan exclaimed at the sight of the vomit all over his seat. She had just puked all over the front of his car. He stopped a good distance from her home, and said to her angrily, "Get out. Get the fuck out!" With her head bent in shame she got out of his car, and watched as he angrily sped away.

Denise removed her heels and walked the rest of the way home. When she got to the house, she quietly opened the door. As she made her way across the den, she was stopped dead in her tracks by the sound of her mom's voice.

"Where were you coming from at this time in the night, young lady?" her mom asked with a worried, pissed off look on her face. After what she thought was the worst night of her life, she had been caught sneaking into her home to put the icing on a bad rotten cake. The question caught her off guard and as she stood there she contemplated whether she should just tell her mother the truth about all that had transpired.

A few months had gone by since the incident had happened with Denise at the party and she was slowly adjusting back to her normal life. Meanwhile, downtown at the police station, her brother, Officer Marc Savy had been assigned a new case by his supervisor. It was an undercover assignment; he would have to college as a student, in an on-going investigation. There had been two murders on campus; both of them were African-American boys and they were both on the same football team.

Everyone had heard about her. Her victims were young African-American college boys in the early twenties. She would take them out, wine and dine them, give them money, sleep with them, then kill them. But no one knew who she was; she was only referred to as "the older woman that he talked so much about." In fact the people of Hunter now had a name for this mysterious woman, the Cougar Killer.

The main suspect of the investigation was a forty–five year old dean of discipline who had for years tried to got the two students who had been killed expelled from school. However they were both from affluent families and their determined parents would always fight her efforts. Now the police believed that she could be the murderer. Maybe she acted out of frustration and spite. However no one was sure that she had indeed murdered the two boys.

As he walked into his first class in the morning as an undercover student, Marc was taken aback by the beauty of his Psychology lecturer.

She was a mature, beautiful African-American woman, probably in her late thirties. But who really cared; she was hot. Marc remembered his real college days, none of his lecturers looked so stunning gorgeous. She wore a black pencil skirt that stopped a few inches above her knees. Her blouse was pink with buttons running down the front; however, the first few buttons to the top were undone, revealing the temptingly, smooth looking beginning of what seemed like perfectly shaped breasts. Her long, clean-shaven legs had a glow and her feet were adorned with a pair of sexy black, pointy-toe stilettos. Marc could hardly keep his jaw from dropping when he saw this drop-dead beautiful diva walk to the front of the class.

His thoughts were interrupted when she called out his name and introduced him to the class at the new transfer student. She then introduced herself as Dr. Lilly Kebabs, his Psychology 101 professor for the fall semester.

As he looked at her, his eyes caught something in hers, and it was like he felt, that she too had felt the same level of attraction towards him. At the end of the two hour class he decided that the best thing to do would be to go over to talk to this woman; after all it would not hurt to just talk. She was very warm and friendly towards him and he almost forgot that he was actually working. Just when he was about to ask her on a date, he caught himself, and instead, asked her whether she would be able to tutor him.

He explained that psychology had never been his forte and since he had missed out on so much class his parents were willing to pay for tutors to help him to catch up. She was a little hesitant at first but finally she agreed and they arranged a time and rate for the sessions.

That afternoon he snuck into the dean's office to do a quick search to see whether he could find any evidence that could link her to the crimes. His hands searched the drawers of her desk, and suddenly he felt something way to the back of one of the bottom drawers. It was a very sharp letter opener. One of the students had been stabbed several times with a letter opener. Could this be the murder weapon? He thought to himself. He placed the object in a clear plastic bag and hid it in his back pocket as he made his way out of the office.

As Marc made his way to her on that Sunday afternoon he was eager to see where this woman he had been crushing over lived. It had been about a month since he first began receiving tutoring from Dr. Kebbs, and although he had not previously like that course, her passion for it was slowing making him enjoy taking that class again.

She was so mature, so knowledgeable, and so beautiful. He would sit there, just staring at her cute, shaped-pink lips with her perfect row of bright, white teeth. Today, since the university library was closed for spring break, she had said he could come over to her home for a tutoring session. As he pulled up in the driveway he took one last peep at her text message. "The gray house to the left, along

Richardson Lane, next to the Laundromat," the text read. He rolled down his window and saw the Laundromat in the corner of his eye, and the house was painted gray. He was definitely at the right house.

After two knocks she opened the door with a smile on her face. This was not the Dr. Kebbs that he was used to seeing. She looked so much more relaxed and there was not a trace of her usually mature, uptight look. She wore black leggings, a white T-shirt and her hair looked amazing as it flowed down her back.

"Come in," she said as she welcomed him in with her outstretched hand and a smile on her face. As he walked in, his eyes scanned the place and he complimented her on how exquisite the interior design of her house was. She smiled at his compliments, and told him that she had done it herself during the summer vacation last year.

As they sat down at the round desk in her home office, Marc decided that there would be no better time than this to get to know her better. He asked about her husband what he did. To his relief she informed him that she was not married; in fact, she was actually divorced, and he had left her for his younger secretary.

"What a fool," Marc gasped as he lost control of his tongue. They continued to talk without doing any psychology work. Maybe it was the environment, or maybe it was the fact that they were both two mature, lonely adults, dancing around the issues that they really wanted to know about each other. Soon, Marc found himself getting a hard on under the table. He looked down at his crotch in amazement. How could she do that? They were just talking about life. She must have noticed when he looked down at his crotch, because the next few moments happened really quickly and came as a complete shock to Marc. She pulled his chair away from the desk and sat on his lap. Although Marc had dreamed about his moment from the first time he had laid eyes her in the classroom, he wanted to make sure this was what she wanted.

Her sweet lips met his and their tongues danced together to the desires of their souls. Their kiss was wet and passionate, and they were both getting really hot and wild. The momentum of the movements of their lips increased as they now practically ripped away each other's clothing. He had rolled down her leggings and pulled off her T-shirt and was now caressing her round, brown nipples with his tongue. She flung her head back and moaned out loud asking him to kiss them harder. She did not have to ask him a second time. He took the nipples in his mouth and pulled on them with a good strong suction, releasing them to gently flick his tongue over them and then grabbing them again with his strong sucking. She moaned, and her body quivered as Marc enjoyed the taste of the nipples that he had been dying to kiss while he was in class. He closed his eyes and indulged in a few minutes of sucking her tits.

Dr. Kebbs ground her bare wet pussy against his raw dick, and he wanted nothing more than to thrust his dick inside her pussy. Using both hands to grip her body weight, he lifted her and seated her down on his long, hard dick. As her pussy glided down on his erection, he could feel her juices making their way down his full dick. He groaned out with pleasure. This was so much more than what he thought it would be. Her pussy was warm and moist, and as he embraced her tightly. He could see a tattoo running across the top of her ass, just below her spine. She was a wild thing, he thought to himself, as he began thrusting his dick upwards inside of her. Each thrust caused her body to jolt and she calmed down a little and glided her wet cunt back along his full length. He wanted more, he needed more of her and so, he gently caressed the nape of her neck with his tongue.

She went wild and was urgently grinding and bumping her wet pussy against his hard dick; her breasts bounced back and forth as she closed her eyes and enjoyed the ride.

"Ohhhhhh," she moaned in a high pitched voice as if she were singing in a choir. She moaned some more and the moaning mixed with her rhythms on his dick increased his desire for her. He grasped her narrow waist and gently used it to rock her body back and forth as he worked his dick deeper inside her moist center. She moaned louder and he captured her lips with his and transferred his desire to her. They fucked for what seemed like hours and just when it seemed like he was about to lose his mind over this woman and her pussy, they both summited their climax together. Their juices exploded and they were left exhausted yet hungry for more of each other.

As Jonathan left of the grocery store, he accidently bumped into her. His eyes immediately caught her and he could see that she was a mature, well-seasoned woman. Although he had never been with an older woman, if ever it were to happen, he would want to be with someone like her.

"That's ok, you don't have to apologize," she said to him in the softest, most gentle voice he ever heard. He quickly dropped down to the ground to help her pick up the things that had fallen out of her grocery bag when they had run into each other. He asked her if he could walk her to her car. She did not hesitate and they had a nice, friendly chat as they made their way through the parking lot. She offered him a ride to campus and he happily took her up on her offer. If he refused the ride, he would have had to wait for the university shuttle that travelled every two hours. His car was down at the repair shop and the other rides that he could have gotten were... dead.

It had been a few months since Derrick and Trey had both been found dead on campus. Derrick had been found naked in his dorm room by a maintenance man and Trey's body had been discovered in the back alley behind the cafeteria. Both of their murders had gone unsolved and the police believed that they were both killed by some mysterious woman. Jonathan's thoughts about his dead friends were interrupted when the woman mentioned that she had to pick something up at this restaurant.

She offered to buy him something, which he did not refuse. She pulled up in the parking lot of the restaurant and disappeared into the restaurant building. When she returned she had several bags of food in her hand. She got into her driver's seat and leaned over to the back seat to put the stuff in the back.

Just as she was turning her head back to the front, he was turning his head round to ask if she needed help. Once again, they bumped heads. "We really needed to do something about this, we keep bumping into each other," she said in a seductive voice. Upon hearing this Jonathan seized the opportunity to fulfil one of his greatest desires. Right there in the parking lot they began kissing each other; their tongues were hot and wild, dancing with passion.

Meanwhile, back at his apartment, Marc received a call from the lab where he had sent the letter opener to be fingerprinted, to see whether they would match those found at the scene of the crime. "Sorry Marc, it's not a match. This dean could not have done this, unless she hired someone else," his co-worker informed him.

Although he would never try to put an innocent woman behind bars, Marc was a bit frustrated. It had been months and just when he found some evidence and felt like he was about to close the case, he hit a rock and was back at the drawing board. So far, they knew she was a woman - an older woman – but, who could it be?

A shiver ran down his spine, as the name Dr. Kebbs crossed his mind. No. It could not be her, she was such a calm, gentle, attractive woman. What would be her motive? Why would she kill her students? Then again, his fear heightened because too often in the past, he had discovered that the most calm and gentle people could turn out to be the most deadly killers. These thoughts made him cringe and he could not even stomach the thought of having slept with a cold-blooded murderer. The more he thought about it, the more positive he became that she was the killer. He took a seat at his table and tried to plan his next move. So far both the boys killed were on the football team. They were both close friends and were very popular. He began thinking, what if there was a next victim, who would it be?

Then it hit him, Jonathan... something. He would be the ideal target. He was the captain of the football team, very popular and also he had been best friends with the two guys that had been murdered. Marc sprung up from his seat. He needed to confront Dr.Kebbs and got a confession out of her, before she killed her third victim. He rushed outside and sped off to her home.

Jonathan was in pure ecstasy, this woman knew exactly how to got his body aching for more. She ran her tongue wildly along his naked body. She was so skillful at what she was doing. Years of experience, he presumed. Their kisses were full of passion; it was unlike anything he ever felt before. She used her tongue and found his youthful erect dick. She grabbed hold of it and without warning her tongue was lavishly licking and sucking it. It felt so good, so unbearable, that he wanted to cry out for his momma.

"Oh shit," he groaned as he took hold of the back of head and pushed it up forward on his dick, causing her to took the entire thing in her mouth. Although he was young, Jonathan had the dick of a mature man. It was well formed and full length and body. The woman almost gagged in her effort to continue sucking the entire dick in one mouthful.

While she was devouring his dick with her hot, passionate tongue, she had managed to get her hands around his tender balls. As she sucked his dick with her tongue, her fingers gently fondled his balls. For Jonathan, this was one of the most amazing feelings. He could tell that the feeling was mutual; she made moans of pleasure where she had him in her mouth. He slipped two fingers inside her moist, veteran pussy. A pleasurable moan escaped her lips. He used this as a signal that she was prepared for his dick down there. He made his way to the back seat and invited her to join him on his dick.

Her pussy came crashing down on his dick, like a chocolate volcano. Her sweet juices made their way down his dick as she rode him like the pro that she was. He found himself for the first time in no control whatsoever. Every move she made blew his mind away and her pussy was the best he had ever had. As she rocked her pussy back and forth on his dick, he could feel her pussy walls contracting as her juices poured out of her core. She rode his dick up and down, back and forth, side to side, grinding and rotating on every inch. He flung his head back as he enjoyed the feel of her wet, experienced pussy on his long dick.

As Marc was on his way to see Dr. Kebbs, he could not help but notice a familiar car. He slowed down a little and he could see the shadows of two figures doing something in the back seat.

Who was in the car, and what were they doing in the back seat? His eyes popped open when he realized that the car was rocking and bouncing up and down. It was like they were having sex in the backseat! He dimmed his lights and drove closer to the car, only to realize that just as he had suspected, there were two people having sex in the car.

Suddenly he checked out the license plate number and he realized that he definitely knew the owner of the car. It must be stolen! He tried to convince himself as he moved in closer to put an end to this madness. As he moved closer, all of a sudden, the figure that was on top riding lifted their hand in the air. But wait, he noticed an object in the person's hand. It looks like some sort of... KNIFE. He pulled out his gun and fired two shots into the air to capture the person's attention so that they would stop. How dare this thief commit such an act in this car?

He banged on the window and there was a struggle and finally a young man, Jonathan, rushed out of the car, with bloody clothes. He was shouting, "She's crazy, man, she crazy!"

"Get out of the vehicle with your hands on your head!" Marc commanded as he had a gun pointed to greet the person.

His jaw nearly dropped, when he saw his mother slowly step out of the vehicle with a bloody knife in her hands. His mother wept, crying loud. "He raped your sister, Marc, him and his fucking friends. They took her and got her drunk and they raped her!" she said angrily with tears in her ears.

Marc stood there, shocked, not able to move one muscle. How could she do this? She was his loving, caring mother. How could she be the Cougar Killer? It seemed like a bad nightmare. Yet, it was all starting to make sense.

Months ago, his sister had come home late. She had been hysterical but he was never told why. His sister did go to school with the boys that were murdered. He knew his mother - she could be a very determined woman when she wanted, but this, oh this was a whole new, unacceptable level. They should have told him. He turned her around, and his policeman duties to uphold the law took over. He cuffed his own mother.

"You have the right to remain silent; anything you say or do may be used against you in a court of law. You have the right to an attorney. If you can't afford one, one would be

given to you by the state."

He put her in the back of his police car and called an ambulance for Jonathan who had been injured with the knife.

The story in the morning paper read;

"Policeman finally apprehends the Cougar Killer; but it was not a stranger, it' was his own MOTHER!"

That night Marc went over to Dr. Kebbs house and she took away all his pain. He had lost his mother but now he had a hot, new lover.

6 AGAINST THE CODE

Mona stormed out on her mother at the very mention of her going to med school. "I don't have to put up with all this! Stop pressuring me, Mom!" she exclaimed in anger, as she slammed the door behind her. She was not the type of a girl that could be easily persuaded to do something against her would. Her parents had a plan for her life that she did not intend to follow.

Mona Chaplan was the only daughter of one of Beverly Hills most prominent African-American couples. She had beautiful curly brown hair, with a heart shaped camera-friendly face. Her mother owned a multimillion-dollar real estate company and her father was a successful maxillofacial surgeon with a huge list of celebrity clientele. Physically speaking, Mona Chaplan was a very attractive woman in her mid-twenties; she had beautiful brown curly hair, sparkling gray eyes and a smile that could charm even a beast. She had attended one of the best universities in the state of California, and had majored in Biology.

However, soon after graduating from college she took up a job in a small restaurant as a pastry chef. As long as she could remember, Mona had always loved cooking, and although her parents wanted her to be a doctor, preferably a cardiologist, Mona always knew she wanted to be a chef. Mona was supposed to be happy because she lived the life that most girls dreamt of, and yet she was miserable. There was one thing that she wanted more than anything else, and that was freedom from her parents.

In Beverly Hills, there were certain standards that must be followed in order to maintain the respect of your neighbors. In the gated community where the Chaplans lived, no one would ever be caught driving themselves; everyone had a personal chauffeur, and the Chaplans were no exception. Mona's driver was Charles, an elderly Caucasian man who had been her chauffeur from the time she was a baby, as her mom would put it. She and Charles had a very close type of father and daughter relationship, and this was also unacceptable in the society where she grew up. It was unheard of for the wealthy people to associate and develop close friendships with common men, or any of their employees. However, Charles had been so much more than a driver to Mona; he had been her friend and confidant to her. As she stepped out the door after the brief argument with her mother, she was relieved to see Charles outside polishing her new 2012 Range Rover SUV.

"How come you're always around when I need you, Charles?" she wondered.

"Yeah I know, right, what would you do without me," he said jokingly. "Going out, I suppose?" he asked her.

"Yep, to the mall," she replied and got into the vehicle quickly, not allowing him to open the door for her. She never liked when he did that, and would always tell him that she was capable of opening the door herself, but he would always reply saying, "A gentleman ALWAYS gets the door."

Charles took her around for the day – to the mall, and then to lunch at her favorite restaurant; and later back to the house for her to get ready for work. Every afternoon he would drive her to work and pick her up in the evenings.

Mona could hear her mom's voice on the intercom in her room. She opened her eyes and looked at the time. It was only 8:00 am. She walked over to the device, pressed the "talk" button and inquired why her mom was waking her up at this somewhat unusual hour.

"There's someone out in the front to see

you. He said he was your driver's nephew, or
something. But I am telling you Mona, this
guy is a mess, and quite frankly, he looks like
a thug, so please go outside and got him to
leave," her mom ordered her in most arrogant
and irritating tone of voice. Mona got out of
bed, went to the washroom to wash her face,
put on her robe and went downstairs to meet
this stranger.

As she opened the front door her jaw
almost dropped to the floor when she saw the
stranger. He was like a diamond in the rough,
all tall and handsome with thick dreadlocks
on his head. He had big hazel eyes and wore a
red polo shirt, which exposed a beautiful
tattoo of a lion that he had on his right arm.
Immediately she was attracted to him, and
she tried hard to control the butterflies in her
stomach.

"Hi, I'm Jamal. Charles sent me over
because he was ill. I work as a taxi driver, for
Courtesy Taxi Service," he said, as he
extended his hand out to greet her.

She looked at him for a while before her
words could come out, "I'm.. I'm Mona, Mona
Chapman, Chaplan," she said as she giggled
nervously after saying her name wrong.

She invited him to come in as she called
Charles on the phone. She realized that she
had several missed calls and even a voicemail
from him informing her that he was ill. She
called him back, and told him that he could
take the week off to get better. She knew that
Charles was a good worker, and that he would
never send anyone to drive her if he did not
trust that person completely.

She took him to the back garage where her cars were parked and showed him all three of her cars that he would drive her around in: an SUV, a convertible and a Chevy truck. Each one was used in different days; never did she use two different vehicles on the same day. Jamal stood there with a smile on his face; he did not understand why this young woman had three different vehicles and even rules as to when they would be used.

Mona mentioned that she worked as a chef, which almost made him crack up when he heard that. "A chef!" he cried in amazement. To him, she seemed like a spoilt rich brat and not like a chef at all. Did she think this was all just some sort of joke? There were thousands of people who really need a job, and here she was with all her money, taking the job that some less fortunate person could have had. He did not know her but he already disliked her; he had very little respect for greedy wealthy people. Mona added that she did not have a fixed schedule, and that she would need to be able to reach him 24/7.

"I'm a very busy woman, and I need a reliable chauffeur that I could count on,". she said to him. He heard those words differently, "I'm a wealthy whore, who parties all night, and I need to have a driver pick me up when I got drunk and wasted at my parties." As they left the garage he thought to himself that Charles must have been crazy to think that he would ever be able to work for this girl. Based on what his uncle had told him, Jamal had pictured that she would be an older and more mature looking woman, who was different from the rest of the crazy wealthy arrogant people from this neighborhood, but she was no different after all.

In fact he was disappointed to see that she was a party animal barely in her twenties. She told him that they had to go shopping later in the morning; she had this charity event to attend and needed to buy an outfit. Then in the afternoon he had to drop her off to work, and then come pick her up in the night.

Mona told him that Charles normally waited for her to get ready outside in the car, but that he could come in and wait for her inside. Jamal also decided to wait outside while she went in to get ready for the day. He waited, and waited, and waited. Finally when she came outside he was shocked to see how different she looked. Everything about her looked different. She had her hair pulled back neatly in a ponytail, and wore a beautiful pink summer dress with white wedge heels. He could not believe how she had transformed into this beautiful lady.

He tried to force himself to look away, but he couldn't – she looked stunning. He went around the car to open the door, but before he could, he felt her soft hands on his hand, and as he looked up at her, she said to him, "You don't have to worry about opening the door for me, okay?"

In that brief moment he could had sworn he felt strong attraction between Mona and him. He brushed off the feeling, and drove her to the boutique.

That night when he came to pick her up from work, she was belligerent, and he could smell the alcohol on her breath. He was upset; he hated people who drink to the point of becoming intoxicated.

It just took him back to his horrible past before he was adopted, when his biological parents would come home drunk and psychically abuses him. He tried hard to ignore her, but his emotions got the best of him, and he pulled up on the side of the road and for a moment completely forgot that she was his employer.

"Now listen to me you spoilt brat, I ain't got time to be dealing with your drunk ass!" he said to her in a firm authoritative tone of voice.

She denied being drunk and asked him to take her to the club. However he had decided that the only place he would take her right now was her home.

When they arrived outside her house, she did not want to got out; he literally had to carry her out of the car, and then took her upstairs to her room. His heart raced as he climbed the stairs in fear that her parents might see him, and assume that he had something to do with her drunken condition.

She showed him the door to her room, and he entered and placed her on her huge king size bed. Her room was by far the largest bedroom he had ever seen in his life; it looked like a suite of a luxurious hotel. As she lay on the bed he looked at her, and in some way felt sorry for her, because he could sense that she was a very unhappy person. He was about to leave when she called out to him and begged him to stay with her.

"I can't stay here, your parents would kill me," he replied.

"No-oo," she said in a childish tone of voice. "They're away on business. Please, I am scared. Stay with me! I lost my job," she lamented.

His heart began to soften towards her, and as he looked at her exhausted body on the bed, he realized that he was somewhat attracted to her. He sat in a chair by the bed and waited for her to fall asleep so he could leave.

Jamal woke up to the sound of a woman's voice on an intercom. He opened his eyes and, to his dismay, he was still in Mona Chaplan's room. He had fallen asleep on the chair next to her bed. As Mona woke up, she thought she was dreaming when she saw Jamal at her bedside. She was attracted to him, and as he got up off the chair reality hit her when she heard the sound of her mother's voice on the intercom.

If there was one thing that was not allowed in her home, it was to bring over a guy. Her mom would probably call the cops if she found Jamal in the room. She looked outside. It was bright and sunny, and the gardener was outside along with her dad. She had to sneak him downstairs and out in the back where no one could see him. "I'll be down for breakfast in a minute," she replied on the intercom.

"My mom will kill me if she saw you in here," she said nervously. "I'm going downstairs. I'll be back with something to eat and then we're going to sneak you out of here. Okay?" she informed him as she was leaving him in the room, ensuring that she locked the door behind her.

As she walked downstairs, her head felt like it was about to explode. She had a terrible headache, and did not want her mom to suspect anything. She quietly slipped into the kitchen and took her breakfast tray. Just as she was about to leave the kitchen, her mom turned around from where she had been standing in front of the kitchen sink and saw her. "Oh Mona, darling, you look horrible! Are you feeling okay?" she asked.

"I'm fine, Mom," she hastily replied as she made her way back upstairs with the food. Her mother knew that Mona was not a morning person, so she carelessly continued what she had been doing.

When she entered the room, Jamal was sitting on her bed with his shirt unbuttoned. Mona could see his perfect abs, and she instantly wanted to explore the rest of his body. "I got you some breakfast," she told him as she handed him the tray. He was so worried that he did not even have an appetite, and she noticed that. "Don't worry about anything. You'll be out of here in a minute, just eat something first," she said in a calm, soothing voice. "Let me take a quick shower, and by then, my parents would be gone to work."

Now, Mona had an opportunity to be quite

a temptress, and she was determined to have Jamal today, in her bed. She slowly walked over to her closet, and pulled out a sexy pink summer dress that was hidden deep inside her huge walk in closet. Then in her drawer she picked a matching pink lace bra and thong.

Jamal's eyes popped out when he saw her placing her underwear on the bed next to him. "What was she trying to do," he thought to himself. Mona began apologizing about her actions last night while she began to undress as if she was speaking to her mom or her best friend. Once naked, she headed to her bathroom, and told him that he could shower when she was done.

Jamal's dick started throbbing when he saw her perfect naked body and he tried hard to control the impulses. "Jamal separates work from play," he thought out loud, as he tried to suppress the urge to follow her into the shower.

After a while Mona got out of the shower naked and Jamal could see tiny drops of water dripping down her skin. She walked over to where he was seated on the bed and sat on his lap facing him. Jamal was too shocked to move a muscle. "Now I could tell from the erection in your pants that you want me, so why didn't you come join me in the shower?" she whispered in a seductively soft voice as she gently caressed his earlobe with her tongue.

Jamal swallowed hard as he tried to answer the question. "I... I don't want to do anything to, to..." he groaned as she ran her tongue down his bare chest, "to lose my job."

"You won't lose your job, trust me," she promised while she ran her hands and her tongue down his body to the buckle of his belt. She looked up at him as she unbuckled the belt and explored the core of his manhood.

Mona was very pleased when she felt his long hard dick. She needed to taste it in her mouth, and even more, she needed to feel it inside her. She pulled out his big dick, and gently caressed it with her tongue. She put her mouth around the head of his dick and then swallowed it in its entirety in quick rapid movements, going up and down on it with her mouth. Jamal groaned with pleasure engrossed in sensations that he felt running through his entire body and that were almost too much to handle. Mona was also enjoying the experience and was pleased that he quivered at her touch.

"Wait! Wait! This was wrong! We can't!" he tried to convince both her and himself, but her mind was made up. She wanted him badly. When he realized that he could not stop her with her deviously delicious plan, he caved in and began to stroke her nipples gently as she sat between his legs sucking his dick. Mona was thrilled to see him actively participating and she slowly stood up, and using her hand on his chest gently pushed him onto her bed. She removed his pants and gave him a long hard suck before mounting his hard dick. Once on top of him, she began bouncing her pussy back and forth on his dick. She could feel his hard cock jamming hard, against the walls of her pussy.

She moaned loud, "Oh God! Yeah!" as she enjoyed the sensations that exploded throughout her body. Her two huge breasts bounced up and down, as she used her pussy to make small circular motions on the tip of his dick. He went wild with pleasure and his groans were long and scruff.

"You like this pussy don't you," she murmured, as she began to increase her momentum. He grabbed her breast with his mouth and sucked it hard. She shrieked with pleasure, and the sensations they felt were earth shattering. "Oh baby! Oh God! I'm going to cum!" he shouted as he gripped her waist firmly, as if to ensure her pussy stayed on his dick. He began launching his dick upwards inside her and after a several long hard thrust they both climaxed together. Their explosion was so intense that they could feel tiny spasms at the core of their togetherness. Her body collapsed on his and they lay in the bed exhausted and surprised at what had just happened.

He looked into her brown eyes, and for the first time felt like they had a real connection.

"What?" she asked him smiling.

"You're beautiful, that's all," he replied.

"Well, you're quite handsome yourself," she replied as she kissed him on the forehead. In that moment, Jamal realized that he had been attracted to her from day one. The strong feelings of dislike that he had towards her were actually his way of masking the attraction he felt. He gently kissed her soft lips and then sat up on the bed. "So what do you had planned for today?" he asked her.

"Well, I was thinking that we could just hang out together. Tonight's the benefit that I have to go to, so I was thinking of going to get my hair and nails done for tonight," she replied. Mona wanted to put all these things on hold and just savor the moment with him, but she feared that he acted in the heat of the moment and was not interested in dating her. After they got dressed, she finally picked up the courage and asked him the question burning in her mind.

"Um, I have a quick question," she said nervously, "Are you seeing anyone right now?"

Jamal was somewhat surprised when he heard her question. He was normally the one asking this. He was impressed at her boldness, and he smiled at her as he replied. "Not at the moment. Why do you ask?"

Mona knew it was the twenty-first century, and these days, when a woman saw a man that she wanted, she went after him. However, she genuinely liked this guy and did not want to scare him or mess things up, so she picked her words very carefully before giving him an answer.

"Well, I was just thinking, you know, I guess you've seen, that I'm kinda into you, you know," she said trying to find the courage to come straight out and just say what was on her mind. "I kinda like you, so I was thinking, that maybe, we could get together, you know, like be together." She finally uttered the words and took a deep breath waiting for him to reply. Jamal was at loss for words. He had definitely felt the attraction that after making love was even bigger, but he doubted whether he was ready to got into any sort of relationship with her. She was very wealthy and independent, and that was a little intimidating for him. However, he had always been a guy who loved challenges, and he saw this as an excellent opportunity to let his guards down, and date someone he would not usually date.

"Maybe this time he would fall in love and things would actually work out," he thought to himself. He looked at her, closely before giving her an answer, as he was trying to scare her, and then replied, "Yeah, I don't mind being with you." Mona's heart leaped with joy as she heard him.

The day went by quickly and soon it was evening time, and Jamal rang the doorbell as he came to pick her up to take her to the charity event. His jaw dropped when she opened the front door. She looked stunning in a sheer silver dress with a deep V-cut. His eyes run up and down her body; he got an erection just from watching her stunning figure and her temptingly beautiful cleavage of a caramel tone. As he drove her to the event, he could not help a slight feeling of jealousy coming over him, since he feared that one of the men at the event might try to get her attention and she would forget the passion they had shared this morning.

"You look beautiful," he said to her as he

opened the door for her to get out when they reached their destination.

"Thank you," she replied, leaned in and gave him a soft kiss on his lips. He grabbed her closer and kissed her long and hard. Mona almost forgot that she had somewhere to be. The entire evening she could not stop thinking about Jamal and wondering what he was doing.

She did not wait for the event to end. Half way during the evening she picked up her cell phone and called him to come pick her up. He was there in less than ten minutes, and as they drove home they engaged in an interesting conversation about her life. Mona told him about her parents, her past relationships and why they had not worked out.

"I feel like I am living the life that my parents want me to live. Can you believe my mom had jeopardized every single one of my past relationships," she complained to him with sadness in her voice. He pulled up in an empty parking lot, and put down the top of her black Mustang convertible. They both got out of the car. She placed herself on the hood of the car as they spoke for what seemed like hours. The stars in sky sparkled as they enjoyed a beautiful evening; it seemed like the more things they shared, the closer they became. Jamal could not take his eyes off of her, and he gave in to the urge to kiss her. As he drew closer to her, he spread her legs and planted a soft kiss on her tender lips. Her tongue grabbed his and they began devouring each other in a series of passionate kissed. As they kissed, his dick became aroused and without evening thinking twice he ripped her panties off exposing her pink wet pussy.

"You wet," he said to her in amazement as he stroked her pussy with his fingers. She started moaning with pleasure. He came in closer to her, pulled out his erect dick and shoved it in her warm inviting pussy.

She shrieked with pleasure licking her lips as he began fucking her on the bonnet of her car. He was not too rough with her, and as he increased his strokes, the passion that they felt for each other heightened. They were carelessly ripping off each other's clothes as they gave in to their desires. She held onto him tightly and enjoyed the ecstasy of his dick going deep and hard inside her tight pussy.

"Oh, yeah! Yeah!" she moaned out loud, as he banged his full manhood into her. He held her legs up high in the air as he relentlessly re-entered her pussy with his huge dick. She moaned and moaned with pleasure. He too was enjoying the feeling of her hot wet pussy on his dick. He could not control himself any longer; he shoved himself deep inside her and she jerked backwards. "Easy there, big boy", she muttered with a smile on her face. He smiled back, as he wiped the sweat that was dripping off his face. He continued thrusting his dick with long slow strokes, and then increased the speed as he got deeper inside her.

"Oh shit! Yeah! Oh yeah! OOO!" he groaned as he exploded inside her. She too had been bursting with pleasure, and climaxed together with him. They both looked deep into each other's eyes, while their juices streamed like a fountain out of her.

When she got home all she could think about was Jamal and the events of the day. She could not believe that she had experienced such pleasures from this guy and all in the same day. At the moment she did not care what her parents thought; she knew she wanted to be with Jamal.

Mona and Jamal continued spending time together, and soon they started hanging out together in public. It had been a few months since they first got together, and so far, Mona had managed to keep their relationship hidden from her parents.

However things were about to take a violent turn. It was a cold winter evening and she had just got through talking to Jamal on the phone when her mom burst into her room, screaming and shouting at her.

"How could you Mona? A taxi driver! You, here, sleeping with the help! It's UNACCEPTABLE! I WON'T HAVE IT, MONA!" Mona looked surprised at her mom, an older woman in her fifties who acted like a spoilt high school brat.

"Mother, I am not going through this with you again. You need to accept Jamal. He is a good guy," Mona replied in a firm calm voice.

"Listen to me, young lady! I would not stoop to your level! If you choose to continue seeing this guy, we will cut you off from your inheritance, and I'm serious! We just want what's best for you, and it did not look good for you to be parading the streets of Beverly Hills with a nobody!"

Mona stared at her mother trying to control her temper. She wanted to get her to see that what she and Jamal had was real, but it felt like she was fighting a losing battle.

"Mom, you are entitled to your own opinion, but I love Jamal and you coca'tuld't change that! We're gonna be together," Mona exclaimed.

"Why are you doing this to me? Why are you going against everything that we taught you? There are standards and codes that we follow here! Why are you breaking them? Why must you try to go against everything we had taught you?" her mom shrieked in a voice filled with sadness and emotion.

"I don't care about your stupid standards and codes! This is my life!" Mona exclaimed, and as she got up to leave the room she felt a hard smack on the right side of her face. Mona could feel a burning sensation on her face, and immediately burst into tears and ran out of the room. She hysterically called Jamal on the phone. She needed to get away from her parents and did not want to deal with them anymore.

Jamal took her to his small one bedroom apartment while she was explaining what had happened. He was saddened by the fact that her parents, her mom in particular, disapproved their relationship. He took her hand and gently kissed it.

"I'm always going to be here for you, and I'm never gonna judge you baby," he said softly. Mona knew that despite all the mean things that her mother had said about Jamal, he had a good heart and was a hard worker. She kissed him on his lips and they looked into each other's eyes and felt each other's pain. He gently laid her on his bed, and undressed her. He then slowly caressed her nipples with his tongue, moving from right to left, and then licking each one specifically. Mona moaned with pleasure, but she wanted more, she wanted to feel his tongue inside her.

He moved his tongue slowly down her body, and gently spread her legs. She shrieked when she felt his tongue on her pussy. He licked it and used his fingers to part the two lips and enjoyed her pussy like it was a delicacy.

"Oh baby, I love you," she moaned as he pleasured her with his tongue. After a while, he mounted her and penetrated her wet pussy with his huge cock. She moaned out loud calling his name as he thrust his dick inside her sweet pussy. "Oh, Mona," he groaned as he continued to thrust his dick inside her in long hard strokes. Their bodies moved rhythmically together, and they both moaned with pleasure. His strokes intensified as he felt like he was about to explode inside her, they were breathing hard and moaning loud. Finally, they climaxed together, and their bodies collapsed on the bed, exhausted from all the fucking.

"I love you, Jamal, and I don't care what my parents say," Mona exclaimed as she looked deeply into his eyes. He could feel the sincerity in her voice.

"I love you too Mona and I am going to do whatever it takes to get along with your parents."

The following morning when Mona got up, she went to the kitchen where Jamal was preparing breakfast. The smell of bacon and eggs made her nauseous and she barely made it to the bathroom. She threw up like she had never done in her life. She did not quite understand, she had not eaten anything yet, she was not drunk from the previous night, she just did not know what was wrong.

Just as she sat on the floor with her head in the toilet bowl, throwing up, Jamal walked in saying "If I didn't know any better, I would think you were pregnant." She looked up at him. That was absurd. "Pregnant, no. Why would you even think something like that?" she replied.

"Well for starters, your boobs were bigger and more tender, you have put on a little weight, and now you throw up in the morning," he replied with a smile on his face. Mona thought about what he had said for a minute, and it soon came to her. She WAS pregnant indeed. All the signs had been there, but she chose to ignore them. In fact she had been feeling nauseous very frequently recently, and she had put on some weight.

"Let's got a test," she said to him eagerly.

Jamal put on some clothes and run to a store that was about five minutes away from his apartment. When he got back, she immediately took the test. After three minutes the test only confirmed their assumptions. They were both ecstatic when they saw the results and jumped for joy, but their joy was cut short when she remembered that she would had to break the news to her parents.

Mona had always been pro-life, and abortion was not even an option for her, and as for Jamal he was totally against adoption, although he had been adopted. Therefore, they decided that they would keep their baby; after all they were two adults who were in love with each other. Mona called her mom on the phone to break the news. She had decided that if her mom did not accept the baby, then she would not go home. When her mother heard her voice, she began apologizing about her violent behavior, "I never meant to hit you, Mona. I'm so sorry!"

"I know, but I'm calling because I'm pregnant, mamma," Mona said, and waited eagerly to hear what her mom would say.

There was a brief moment of silence and then, she heard her mom burst into tears, "Mona! Oh my God! Please come home! Please! I don't care about your boyfriend! I'm gonna be a grandma!" Mona's mom had always wanted a grandchild, but she never expected that the baby's father would be an average guy. Although she was initially disappointed with her daughter's choice of lover, she was overjoyed at the thought of having a little baby around the house. "You remind me of myself when I was young. You just go with your heart doing the unexpected, against all the codes," her mom said laughing.

Mona was relieved to hear her mom; it cheered her up. This baby has been just what her family needed to accept Jamal. When she got off the phone Mona looked at Jamal with a smile on her face and said "We're having a baby."

Jamal hugged her tightly; he vowed to protect and provide for both her and their baby.

"I love you Mona Chaplan," he said with a huge smile on his face. In the end everything worked out great for the two people from different classes of society, they went against all the codes and found some deep-rooted love for each other.

7 HER WEEK IN HEAVEN

"Ladies and Gentlemen, the captain have now turned off the seatbelt sign, you may take this time to move around and use the lavatories," their flight attendant said in a clear, precise tone of voice. It had been about half an hour since taking off, and the captain had just turned off the seatbelt sign. Kandi and Marcus Ellis sat on the plane eagerly anticipating their arrival to the beautiful island of Barbados. Kandi was dressed in a beautiful white wedding gown, while Marcus still wore his black tux.

They had gotten married a few hours before they boarded their flight from Dallas, Texas, to Kingston, Barbados. While most passengers unbuckled their seatbelts and slouched back in their seats with their headphones on, a few made their way down the narrow aisle to the washroom. Kandi looked over at her husband with lustful eyes; he had been everything she ever wanted in a man. His chocolate brown complexion matched hers, his smile captivated her heart, and his strong arms were always there to embrace her. The seat next to them was unoccupied and a tiny smile formed in the corners of her mouth as she moved her hands to his crotch area. Without noticing what his wife had been up to, Marcus, jolted back a little when he felt her instant firm grip on his crotch. He looked at her and she could tell that he was probably a little uneasy about her unorthodox display of public affection.

Being the temptress that she was, Kandi tightened her grip and tried to work the zipper to get to his dick. He tensed up a little and she gave him a little wink and used her sweater to cover her wandering hand. "Relax baby, I just want to feel him a little," she whispered in his ear as her fingers made contact with his hidden dick.

He cringed a little as if trying to get comfortable, while she played with his tool. Kandi gripped his dick firmly with her hand, and stroked it up and down, up and down until he could feel it stiffening up. His nerves went wild as he tried to contain himself and not allow any groaned to escape from his lips. But Kandi was getting a thrill watching him try to conceal the pleasure of the sensations that she was increasing with every stroke.

The urge to bring her mouth downwards and whip out his huge dick was becoming almost unbearable for her. She soon found herself enjoying the hand job she was giving to him, and the amazing part was now she was undoubtedly horny.

They had not had sex for a week for fear that it might bring bad luck for the wedding; in fact, and they had not really seen much of each other that week either. In their attempt to follow family traditions they had stayed away from each other, making their desire to be together greater than ever before. They were like two caged beasts, about to be released into the wild.

After a few minutes Kandi pulled her hands out of his pants, and looked towards the direction of the washroom. She saw the green unoccupied sign on the door and she scanned the plane carefully observing what the passengers and flight attendants were doing. Some people were sleeping; others were watching TV, while the flight attendants were stationed in the front.

"Let's go to the bathroom. I'll go first, wait about a minute and then come; I'll be waiting," she whispered to him. She got up and made her way to the tiny bathroom and waited for him. Those sixty seconds seemed like an hour, and she was now crossing her fingers hoping that he would hurry up. A few short taps on the door and she opened the door to let him in. Once inside Kandi captured his full lips with hers and her hungry tongue darted to explore the inside of his mouth. Their kisses were filled with desire, and their panting could be heard as they worked frantically to satisfy each other right there in the bathroom of the plane. Her hands roamed freely all over his body, while he found a path up her short white dress to her silky thighs.

His fingers found that her bridal lingerie

was saturated from the arousal brought on by their kisses, and his kiss deepened as he realized how wet she was.

"Oh God baby, I want you so bad," he groaned as he moved his lips down the nape of her neck, all the while his fingers stroked her wet pussy. Kandi's body responded well to his touch, and every time he stroked her flesh she moaned softly. Marcus braced her up against the bathroom wall, and proceeded to release his huge cock from his underwear. He unzipped his pants dropping them down to his ankles. Now free from his most restricting clothes, he proceeded to rid her of her panties. With a slight tug, the thin strings of the thong she had been wearing tore apart, and he looked at her before flinging it to the corner.

As she looked down at her panties, her eyes caught a glimpse of his erect penis. He had a huge, long cock. It was slightly darker than his complexion and it had a rough texture, due to several bulging veins running across it. Marcus lifted her right leg up with her back against the wall, and he directed his huge erection upwards inside her wet pussy. Her body stiffened as she focused all her energy on trying to accommodate his long dick. He continued driving his penis into her, until the entire thing was inside of her. She held on to his arms, as he rammed her hard with his dick. The harder he fucked her, the more she begged him not to stop. The thrusts were long and steady at first, but then as their passion got stronger, so did his thrust. He was slamming his dick violently inside her pussy as she held on to him. Her pussy was like a fountain and as he fucked her, her juices covered his hard dick. He groaned when he felt the slightly hot liquid flowing down his dick. "You're gonna drive me crazy with that shit," he grunted as he gave her several hard thrusts.

She moaned as she could feel the building intensity of her impending climax. "Oh God, Oh God!" he groaned.

And with that his thrust became even harder than before; he was like a man controlled by his dick. Her pussy was going wild and as he fucked her in the bathroom she felt every inch of his long dick inside of her. She gripped his arms and clenched her teeth as she finally summited her climax.

He too, after a few seconds, groaned as he exploded a sea of hot cum inside her damaged pussy.

There was a knock on the door of the bathroom. "Is someone in there?" a voice from the other side of the door asked. Kandi and Marcus looked at each other, as they stood there with cum dripping. They were busted!

What an experience they had on the plane, Kandi thought to herself. In a few hours they had gotten into so much mischief, from giving her husband a hand job, to fucking in the bathroom, to getting busted by the flight attendant. As they got off the plane, Kandi was happy to be moving past the most embarrassing experience of her life. When they had gotten busted in the bathroom, the flight attendant had informed them that they could have gotten fined for indecent exposure, and she required that they took seats in separate areas for the duration of the flight. Kandi did apologize to her, telling her that they were newlyweds and were just being adventurous. But the older woman was not moved or impressed.

"Ah! Barbados," Kandi said as she stepped off the plane. She removed her sunglasses and took a deep breath of the clean, crisp Caribbean air. As she looked over at her husband she could see that he too was enjoying the moment. "Mr. and Mrs. Ellis," was written on a poster that a young man was holding upwards a few inches past his head.

"This must be our taxi driver," she said as she led her husband in the direction of the young man. They would be staying at the Crane Hotel, one of the best hotels on the island of Barbados. When she was looking for a resort, she was impressed by the number of positive reviews this hotel had. One of the former guests went as far as describing it as 'heaven on earth.' The drive to the hotel was a long one, and by the time they got to the hotel it was already dark.

They were greeted by two very friendly hostesses, and then escorted to the reception area, where they checked-in to the hotel and received their room keys. Then they were taken to their room on a golf-cart. The place was simply divine; the hotels best feature was its unique architectural design. Kandi was happy that she had chosen to stay at this hotel. When they got to their room, they were further impressed with the amazing view that they had from their cozy patio area. "This place must be heaven," she thought as she sipped on a pina colada admiring the breathtaking view of the moon on the ocean.

Her husband was out of the shower, and as she made her way to the shower, she pulled a medium box out of her suitcase. She did not take a very long shower, and when she got out she spent a few minutes in the bathroom putting on some sexy lingerie that she had bought especially for this occasion. She also pulled out the red blindfold and pink fur handcuffs that came along with the lingerie.

"You ready for me baby?" she called out to her husband before opening the bathroom door.

His eyes nearly popped out and he licked his lips when he set eyes on the sexy body walking out of the bathroom. The black, lacy panty and bra set she was wearing was a matched set; the handcuffs and blindfold dangling from her right hand. She watched her husband's naked body as he lay on the bed prepared to receive her. "You look amazing," he whispered to her as he licked his lips again. As she sauntered over to him, she could see his cock was now standing at attention, like it had a mind of its own. She slithered up onto the bed and straddled him to handcuff his hands to the headboard of the bed, and then used the blindfold to block off his vision. Her heart thumped as she tried to remember all the things that she had planned for tonight. After all, this was one of the most special nights of her life.

Taking a block of ice from the small ice tray in their mini fridge next to the bed, several thoughts rushed through her mind.

"Would he enjoy this new technique? Would she be able to do it right?" she wondered. He lay quietly waiting, not knowing what she was up to, since he had been blindfolded.

"Oh shit!" escaped his lips as he jerked back and tried to wiggle his way out of the handcuffs. Kandi had the piece of ice in her mouth, as she gave his dick a long hard suck. He had been caught off guard with the cold ice on his dick. "Shit, that felt good," he groaned.

Kandi's heart skipped with joy, feeling like she now had his permission to continue. She lowered her ice-cold mouth onto his thick cock once more, and this time, used her tongue and the ice in her mouth to caress his erect penis. This made his body go wild and he groaned like a bitch, as she sucked his dick. The added accessories such as the blindfold and handcuffs made her feel even more in control. As she licked his dick, the desire to pleasure him like never before consumed her. Her tongue moved slowly over his dick, and then she worked her way to the head of the dick, making small circular motions around the rim. She then flicked her tongue back and forth on the head, and then finally she used her tongue to trace the length of the veins that run across his dick.

All this while, Marcus was calling out her name, and begging her for more. His dick had gotten to a degree of erection that she had never seen before; it was double the size of anything she was used to seeing with him.

She continued sucking his dick, then licking it, and then sucking it again. She could feel the dick getting harder and harder, until he begun shoving it upwards in her mouth. Somehow, he had broken free of his handcuffs. His hand now grabbed her head, and held it onto his dick while he shoved it upwards into her mouth, causing her to gag. His cock got harder and harder, and the movements increased, finally there was an explosion of hot, salty semen in her mouth. He released a loud groan as he pushed his dick all the way inside her mouth to the point where she felt his long dick choking her.

"Swallow it, c'mon," he said as he gave her two tiny smacks across her cheeks. He did not have to tell her twice, she closed her eyes, and allowed his hot, slimy liquid to trickle down the back of her throat.

"Now, you put on the blindfold," he said, as he tried to fix the broken handcuffs, so he could now pleasure her the way she had pleasured him.

As Kandi lay in the bed naked with her hands handcuffed and her eyes blindfolded, she felt a strong sense of curiosity creep upon her.

"What was he going to do to her?" was the question burning in her mind. She took some deep breaths as she tried to relax. Her attention was swept away when she heard a soft vibrating sound. Almost instantly, she felt the sudden impact of a small vibrator on the tip of her clitoris. As the vibrator moved against her clit, tiny spasms ran through her body like electricity. This was too much to bear! This was the first time she experienced a vibrator, and it was amazing! Her desire increased when she felt two of Marcus's fingers gliding their way upwards inside her wet pussy. This man was wicked! He had a vibrator on her clit, while he used his fingers moving them rapidly up and down in her pussy. Her thoughts were interrupted when she felt his soft hot tongue in her wet cunt.

"Oh my God!" she shrieked, as he worked his tongue back and forth on her inner flesh. In and out, his tongue went, inside her pussy, and then he put down the vibrator for a minute and indulged on her clitoris with his tongue. It was a vicious attack on her pussy and every touch that she felt sent shockwaves through her body.

His tongue was like hot, wicked, and he sucked every inch of her horny pussy, causing her to moan and cry out to God. She got to the point where she could no longer handle the heat and begged him to stop, but he shook his face in her pussy. Her finger dug into the sheets, as her knees trembled at the way he maneuvered his tongue all over her pussy. "Oh my, my," she moaned as she closed her eyes tightly and tried to reach her climax.

"Don't you cum on my face, save that for my dick," he instructed as he pulled his tongue out of her wet cunt.

"Ohhh," she moaned as she felt the full length of his throbbing dick penetrating the wet, flesh between her legs. This man was trying to drive her insane, she thought. He pulled his dick out and then drove it back inside her pussy this time harder than before. Kandi clenched her fists as her toes curled. He was going to fuck the hell out of her and she knew it. His dick felt like a long, hard stick penetrating its way through her most delicate area.

Suddenly his lips were on her lips, and he forced his tongue into her mouth, kissing her passionately as he thrust his dick inside her pussy. With each thrust the suction and passion of his kiss increased, and her body melted under his. She wanted to scream out with pleasure, as the ecstasy that she felt was mind-blowing.

"Oh God baby, that fucking pussy, you don't even know," he said as he began banging his dick, harder and harder inside her.

"Oh Marcus," she moaned as she held onto his shoulders. His dick was so long that she could feel it, deep down within her very soul. The wild kisses were increasing her desire for him. She loved him deeper, deeper than anything. She wanted this dick for the rest of her life, she wanted his cum, she wanted it all inside her, and she wanted his babies. In fact she wanted everything this delicious chocolate man had to offer. She closed her eyes under the blindfold as her pussy now started doing movements on its own. Every thrust he made with his dick, her pussy responded with a contraction, which only made him thrust harder and deeper. His thrusts were so deep and hard that she thought that he had forgotten that her pussy was but a tiny hole. The way he was fucking her right now, it was like he was a monster, destroying her pussy with his big cock. She moaned and pleaded with him to slow down but he did not, gradually he began hitting her g-spot and all the pain was masked by a feeling of supreme, ultimate pleasure.

Kandi, screamed out, "Fuck yea, motha' fucker, God, fuck, shit!" as she climaxed like she had never done before in her life. Marcus' dick went crazy, when it felt the spasms that her pussy made after she squirted on him. And he too closed his eyes, as he drove his dick up inside her as hard as he could. Thrust after thrust, he did, and finally with a huge, mighty thrust, he exploded his hot semen inside of her. Both of their bodies fell crumpled and twisted onto the bed, exhausted from all the action of the night.

The following morning the plan was an island adventure tour for the two of them, but they were so exhausted that they decided to stay in bed for the day. When the evening time came, they went out into the city and enjoyed the night life that the island had to offer. They met some friendly islanders who shared myths about the island with them. One of the islanders told them that it was believed that the ancestors called Barbados 'land of the heavenly spirits' because, they said, the Gods blessed them with a beautiful island. That night when they went back to the hotel they lay in the king-sized bed and just snuggled in each other's arms.

Their vacation was going great but it was about to come to an end. On the final night, Kandi planned a beautiful candlelight dinner for them on the beach. They enjoyed the food and they had a great time enjoying the panoramic views of the night.

The more they spoke about their life and made plans for the future, the more slowly they became aroused and wanted to have each other right there, in the sand on the beach. Kandi had never had sex on the beach so this would be a first, as it was with everything else that they had done on this trip. She was wearing a short, red tube dress that accentuated her divine figure, while her husband wore khaki shorts, and a polo shirt. As they kissed, their bodies got hot for each other. Soon he was moving his tongue all over her body, as she lay naked in the sand. He stopped for a while and paid special attention to her full breasts, caressing each nipple with his tongue. Her pussy was getting wet as he licked, sucked, and occasionally gave tender bites to her nipples. He managed to use her hand to grab hold of his now erect dick, stroking it, guiding her with his hand. As they used their hands and tongues to give each other pleasure, Kandi had the desire to ride his dick.

She tactfully got him to stop fondling her breasts and instructed him to lie down in the sand, taking up the same position that she had been in. He did it without hesitation, and she mounted him, sliding her wet pussy over his erect cock. His eyes brightened up as she now began to ride his cock, up and down, back and forth. Her movements were slowly at first, but when she leaned in to kiss him, his desire increased and so did her movements. She made small rotation movements with her hips, grinding against him. Her upward movements caused her huge breasts to bounce up and down enticingly over his face. Marcus finally propped his back up and grabbed hold of her nipple with his mouth, grabbing the tip of it with his teeth. She moaned out with pleasure as she felt his hot tongue creating magical sensations through its grip on her nipples. "Oh baby, you're gonna...make...me cum...good..." she moaned as she closed her eyes and pushed herself up and down on his huge tool. As she rode him, she tilted her head backwards and could see the moon and stars in the sky. The night air was filled with their moaned and the soft lapping sounds of the waves. This was what she had hoped her honeymoon would be and so much more.

As they fucked, they called out each other's names in the heat of the moment. She rode his cock, and had him begging her for more. "Oh yeah, faster, uh-huh, yeah," he groaned as he grabbed hold of her waist and now used his strong hands to control her movements. He was now slamming her hard on his dick, and she was enjoying every minute of it. She moaned and moaned and her juices flowed and flowed. His dick was dripping with her pre-cum and he slammed it inside her pussy over and over again. He wanted to pleasure her in every way he could, but this was just the half of what he had planned for tonight. Without warning, he lifted her pussy off his cock and stood up. "I wanna hit it from the back in your virgin hole," he said.

She looked at him, shocked. "Why did he want to fuck me in my ass?" she thought. They had tried it once before but it had been so painful they had to stop. She had not even had any lube right now, and she had a feeling that he would try to make her scream and cry all night. Anyways, she thought, it was their honeymoon, and she wanted to please him.

She got on all fours, and popped her ass out toward him. She knew it would be painful and braced herself for the worst. She felt his hand stroke her pussy, moving up and using the juices from her pussy to lubricate her asshole. Then suddenly she felt his hot, tongue licking her ass thoroughly. This was the most amazing feeling ever. His tongue felt hot, wet and delicious on her asshole, he slid it inside the hole and it did not hurt at all, in fact, it felt good... really good. Then she felt his fingers forcing their way inside loosening it up for what was coming. This was a bit tough, but he pulled them out and lubricated her asshole with his saliva and again, caressing it with his tongue.

The next thing she felt was not his tongue, nor was it his finger; it was his long, hard dick, trying to force its way into her ass. The muscles of her anus contracted tightening against the invasion, and she shrieked out in pain.

"Please stop... don't... it hurts," she begged him, but he did not listen. He bent over her slightly, reached around and used his fingers to stimulate her pussy. His fingers rubbed against her clit, and then stroked the inside flesh of her pussy, this made her even wetter than she was. So good was this stimulation, that she almost forgot about his dick making its way into her ass.

A sudden mighty thrust hit her and she nearly leaped forward, in pain, "God Damn!" she shouted, as he grabbed her by her hips, and continued penetrating her ass with his thick cock. She moaned and a moaned in pain, and tears formed in the corners of her eyes.

As he was fucking her ass, he was also stimulating her pussy. Soon enough, the burning pain that had been associated with the thrusts inside her anus, were forgotten, masked by pleasure coming over her as he stroked her clit. She felt like she was on the brink of a mighty explosion. He repeatedly launched his dick inside her ass, tightening the grip he had on her hips. He begun fucking her asshole hard, and this time, she did not ask him to stop - this time she was enjoying it.

Their bodies moved in rhythm together, and they climaxed together, with his cock buried to the hilt in her ass. His semen dripped downwards from her anus, to meet her juices that were flowing from her pussy.

The entire evening was like nothing they had ever experienced together before. This was the better than heaven. They made their way to their room and once again they made love, before falling asleep.

Kandi woke up to the sound of a familiar voice, but it was not that of her husband, it was her mom.

"Mom," she said. "What were you doing here?" she continued as she looked around, trying to understand why she was not in her hotel room. The older woman seated on the bed next to her wiped away the tears that were trickling down her cheeks. "Baby there's, um, there's been an accident." Kandi could not believe her ears, what was her mother was talking about? She knew nothing of an accident.

Her mother held onto her hands tightly, as she explained to her why they were not in a hotel room, but rather in a hospital room. Kandi's fiancé Marcus had been a police officer and the week before his wedding had been shot during a police raid. He had succumbed to his injuries before he could make it to the hospital. The tragedy of his death hit Kandi hard, and she never got over him. It had been exactly one year since his death, and Kandi had spent the night at a bar drinking and wallowing in her sorrow, like she often did. On her way home, she lost control of her vehicle, running off the road and hitting an electrical pole. The accident had put her in a serious coma.

For a solid week now, her mother had been at her bedside, hoping and praying that her daughter would wake up. When she finally did wake up, she had no memory of what had happened. Kandi was in shock upon hearing the news of all what had happened, after all, the last thing she had remembered doing was making love to Marcus.

She burst into tears, "It's not true, Mom," she shouted angrily at her mother. "It's just not true, I was just with him!" she said, as she cried her soul out.

In that moment the doctor walked in and with a worried look on his face he asked, "Why was she crying like this, she needs to stop crying before she went into cardiac arrest." He walked over to Kandi and tried to calm her down, but it was too late. She gripped her chest as if she could not breathe and before the doctor could do anything, she went into cardiac arrest. The team of nurses rushed into the room and they, with the doctor tried everything they could do to resuscitate her, without success. Her mother swayed from side to side, screaming and crying, gnashing her teeth and fell to the floor in the hospital room in a sobbing heap. Kandi was her only child and now she was dead.

Meanwhile, Kandi opened her eyes and tried to tell her mother that she's ok, but she looked and realized that she was back in the hotel room and the love of her life, Marcus, was lying right next to her. A cold feeling comes over her, as she realized that she may be dead.

She woke Marcus up to question him. "Am I dead? Are you dead? What's going on Marcus?" she asked frantically. The look in his eyes gave her all her answers. At first she was sad to find out that she had in fact died, but then again, the past year without Marcus had been like living in hell. She was more alive now than she had ever been. She looked deep into his hazel eyes, and she saw the man that she fell in love with that day, on campus, while they were still in their teens.

There was nowhere else that she would have rather been. This was the love of her life, and without Marcus, she did not feel like she had a life.

"This was the afterlife," he said to her. It was as if he could read her mind. "There were no crashes, no gunshots, and no death here, just us living life the way we had planned, the future that we had planned," he said as he kissed her softly. She looked at him and realized that she did get to go on her honeymoon with him; she had just spent a week in heaven with him. And now that they were together she would spend the rest of eternity with him.

8 ISLAND SENSATIONS

As Marcia paced back and forth in her pink Victoria secrets lingerie and her pink six inch heels, she keeps mumbling to herself. "This was what I got for trying to be a good wife, where the hell was Danny?" she said. It was the evening before their sixteenth wedding anniversary and she had cooked his favorite meal; there was Lionel Richie's music playing in the background, and she was wearing lace underwear.

However, although her husband Danny had said that he was on his way home an hour ago, he was still not home, and even worse, he was not answering his cell phone. Marcia Grey was tall and slender, her skin was the color of light brown chocolate, and she had beautiful, curly, brown hair that fell down her back. She was a high school teacher by profession and had dedicated most of her time towards helping underprivileged children, since she did not had any of her own.

Her husband Danny Grey was a successful lawyer, who worked at one of the top law firms in Monroe, Louisiana, where he and his wife shared a beautiful three bedroom house. Danny Grey was tall and handsome; he had the most beautiful brown eyes and what seemed like the world's most perfect smile. He had beautiful straight white teeth, and could had made lots of money advertising for Colgate toothpaste.

He was of African American descent; however his skin was more of a light caramel complexion, indicating he had Caucasian blood in his family. Marcia and her husband Danny, or Dan as she called him for short, were married for fifteen years and they were just about to celebrate their sixteenth year of being married. She had been looking forward to this anniversary especially because she had gone all out, and planned an extravagant one week trip to the Caribbean.

However, tonight was the night before their anniversary and she wanted to do something special for her husband. When it was about one in the morning, she had still not heard anything from Dan, she was tired and furious, and so she went to bed.

Marcia did not know what time her husband got home, but he was lying in the bed when she got up the following morning. "Happy Anniversary," she whispered, as she gave him a nudge to see if he was up.

It was too early in the morning to start an argument, so she decided she would wait for him to got out of bed and got settled before she confronted him about last night. When he finally got up, as soon as she mentioned the fact that she had been waiting up for him almost the entire night he got upset and took his car keys and stormed out of the house. "I don't had to deal with your attitude," he said as he slammed the door behind him.

Marcia did not know what to do, she felt like she was stuck in a box. They were travelling to Saint Lucia tomorrow, and here Dan was, coming home at odd hours in the morning and then walking out on her. She went upstairs to start packing for what seemed like it would be a tiring trip. Danny did not come home until late that evening, and when he got to the house, he acted like nothing had happened.

"Your bags were already packed, I put everything you would need in there," Marcia said to him, as she zipped up the last bag and pulled it to the corner of their bedroom where the other packed bags were. Danny replied by just nodding his head to acknowledge that he had heard her, then he fixed himself a sandwich and took a beer out of the fridge and sat on the couch watching TV. Marcia tried hard to give him his space; she did not want to start an argument again. She went to the kitchen, had a glass of water and went to bed.

Before going to bed she told him that they needed to be out of the house by five in the morning so he may want to go to bed early tonight. He again just nodded his head at her.

It's the morning of their trip, Marcia jumped out of bed at the sound of the alarm clock, then proceeded to go over to Danny's side of the bed and wake him up so he could got ready.

When they got to the airport, it was about 5:30 am; they checked in their bags at the American Airlines counter and waited to board their eight hour flight from Monroe, Louisiana to Castries, Saint Lucia.

As Marcia sat on the plane, she was happy that she was getting to took this vacation with her husband. "We need this," she thought to herself. They had been married for such a long time, and yet they had no children.

Danny was a workaholic and Marcia was happy to got him away from the office to a secluded resort so they could relax and spend time together, their marriage needed that.

They had no children because Dan had always said he wanted to be doing well in his career before having children. Now it seemed like although he was doing well, he was too busy. Whenever she had brought up the subject of having kids his reply was always: "It's not a good time for us to had a bunch of children running up and down the house, driving us crazy," and he would laugh. She wondered if he was ever going to want any children, or was he going to try to had children when he was retired.

Finally, in what seemed like forever, the pilot announced that they were about to land in Saint Lucia. They heard the flight attendant say, "Ladies and Gentlemen, welcome to the beautiful island of Saint Lucia. The weather here was currently 95 degrees, it was a beautiful day, hope you all had a lovely time here. Thank you for flying American Airlines."

Marcia could hardly wait to got off the plane to see the island, she looked of over at Dan; she could also see the look of excitement on his face.

"Yes," she thought to herself, "We definitely we need this," It had been a while since she saw his face light up like this.

Meanwhile, at the Bronx Christian Fellowship Church, Eric Romain and Karen Johnson, exchange their vows in holy matrimony. As Eric looked at Karen, he couldn't help but think that he had landed one of the most gorgeous black women in New York. Karen looked simply divine, she was smiling with those perfectly white teeth, and she had a beautiful light pink shade of lipstick on that made her lip look all the more kissable.

As he stood there in his tux shaking, he could see a small stream of tears running down her cheeks. He took his forefinger and gently wiped away her tears. He never wanted to see another tear in her eyes. He had loved this woman so much that after dating her for only three months, he knew that she was the one, and he wanted to marry her. Karen was a woman of little drama, very timid and shy, and that was what attracted him to her. Although he was a more wild and loud individual he believed that she would help him become a better person.

"Karen, do you took this man to be your lawfully wedded husband, to love and to cherish, in sickness and in health, till death do you part, as long as you both shall live?" the Reverend Minister asked Karen with his Bible in his hand.

"I do," she replied as she looked at Eric, standing in front her. He looked incredibly tall and handsome, he was well shaved, and his hair was clean cut, with tiny waves running through it. She loved this man with all her heart and there was nothing she would not do for him, she wanted to spend the rest of her life with him. She had dreamed about her wedding day as a child, and she was not disappointed. Today was the happiest day of her life.

As Eric stood there, holding her hands, his eyes moved up and down, admiring how stunning she looked. Her dress was silky white, with small pearly bid decorations on it. It was a tube dress and she had a sparkly diamond necklace draping her beautiful long neck. She had matching diamond earrings and she had a small diamond tiara in her hair. She had not won a veil because she maintained the belief that she did not want any part of her face covered. Eric did not even hear the entire question because he was too mesmerized by his beautiful bride, all she remembered hearing was "... as long as you both shall live?" and the Reverend was looking at him, as if waiting for an answer. "I do," he replied. Then the next thing he remembered hearing was, "You may now kiss the bride. I now pronounce you husband and wife. Ladies and Gentlemen, I present to you Mr and Mrs Eric and Karen Romain." He remembered giving Karen a long passionate kiss, and hearing the "oohs" and "awws" in the congregation.

It was a beautiful ceremony and everyone was coming up to them outside of the church to congratulate them. They thanked everyone for coming and quickly made their way to the car, as they rushed to the airport to catch their two o'clock flight to Saint Lucia for their honeymoon in paradise.

They had a straight eight hour flight from La Guardia Airport, New York, to George Charles International Airport, Saint Lucia. When they finally arrived, it was nighttime. As they looked to the side of the airport, they could see the ocean nearby. They rushed to got their bags, and tried to find the taxi driver that the hotel had sent to pick them up from the airport. Along the ride to the hotel, they watched the other cars drive by, the roads were narrow and winding, they were a bit scared. Karen's heart almost skipped a bit when the taxi driver took a curb while another car was approaching at full speed. Luckily, nothing happened and they arrived safely at the hotel.

They stayed at the Sandals Grande Resort, in the north of the island; it was one of the best hotels in the entire Caribbean region. The staff that greeted at the front of the hotel were very warm and pleasant. They welcomed them with cocktails and warm towels, which the staff said helped one relax after a long flight.

The bellhop took their bags to their room while they went to the front desk to check in. After they checked in, another bellhop took them to their room on his golf cart. Karen stood at the door in amazement when she saw how beautifully decorated their honeymoon suite was. At eight hundred dollars a night, they had received everything they expected and much more; there was a bottle of red wine in an ice bucket on the night stand. The bed was decorated with Hershey's kissed, strawberries, pretty rose petals and other flowers. There was the sweet scent of lavender coming out of the bathroom where a warm bubble bath was waiting with lavender scented candles around the Jacuzzi. The sound of soft jazz music was playing on the radio. The room was warm and inviting. The look on Karen's face was priceless, and Eric knew he had pleased his wife.

They got settled and Eric put in a CD he had brought with him, with all Karen's favorite love songs. He then took off his clothes and went to join her in the Jacuzzi. She looked beautiful; her skin glistened and right then and there, he knew he wanted her. His manhood was throbbing and he began to slowly nibble on her earlobe, he then moved his hands slowing all over her body. He could then feel her hard nipples. He stood up and he wanted her on the bed where he could really had his way with her. He gently scoops her in his arms and places her in the center of the bed. As she lay on her back, he spread her legs and began running his tongue along her legs, starting with her knees and then working his way up. Eric could tell that Karen wanted him; he looked into her eyes, and they were completely dilated and filled with a look of desire. "Do you want me to continue doing this?" he asked, as he used his tongue and stroked her inner thighs.

"Ummm, yes, I do," she moaned in reply to his question. He spread her leg even further, and placed a small pillow under her ass, to prop up her pussy. He then used his finger and parted her pussy lips, beginning to lick each side of her pink flesh.

Her pussy was neatly shaved, pink on the insides and brown on the outside. He began to lick it vivaciously. Then unexpectedly, he gripped onto her clitoris with his mouth, and began to gently suck on it. Karen was now twisting her body as the intensity of these sensations was almost unbearable. Eric gently pulled away while slowly letting go of her clitoris. He brought his head out of the inside of her legs, looked directly into her eyes and told her, "I'm a going to suck that pussy until you cum. I want all of you, I want you to surrender it all to me baby." He moved upward and began to caress her nipples.

He focused his attention on one nipple, licking and sucking it with a rhythm. "Oh, babbyyy, yess... Oh yes, umhum, yessssss," Karen kept moaning with pleasure. Her pussy was throbbing with great desire, and she wanted him to go down on her again. Karen did not even had to say anything, it was like he sensed it. Eric ran his fingers down to her pussy, and it was dripping wet. He almost went wild when he realizes how wet she was.

191

"Baby, you were soo wet," he said as he looked at her with amazement in his eyes. Karen gave a shy smile as she tried to contain herself. "Let me took care of all this juice dripping out this sweet pussy," Eric said as he moved downwards and spread her legs open lavishing her pussy with his tongue.

This time, his tongue was wild and vicious on her pussy, and as he was stroking her pussy, she moaned with more desire in her tone. Eric licked the pussy, he sucked the pussy, he played with her pussy, and he gently bit it. It was clear that he was enjoying himself while driving her crazy. Karen was filled with pleasure as if she was almost ready to explode, her fingers gripped the bed and her ass appears to be lifting itself as Eric increases the pleasure that he was giving her. There was this sweet feeling in her pussy and she never felt anything like this before. Eric passed his tongue back and forth on her clitoris, as if he was licking an ice cream, but with quicker harder licked. He then released his whole tongue inside her pussy, as if he were trying to find some hidden treasure buried deep within her. He gripped her ass as he launched his tongue inside her pussy. Karen could not hold back, it was the sweetest, most intense feeling ever.

"OH MY GOD, BABY!!" she shrieked, "I' gonna cum... I'm gonna cum," she said it twice with more urgency the second time. Upon hearing this, Eric sucked her clitoris and this time, he used his two fingers to finger fuck her, while sucking on her clitoris. Karen went wild when she felt his fingers jamming inside her pussy.

"Oh, yes, baby, oh my God, Eric! Eric !Yes," she shouts as she moved her body now in rhythm with his tongue and fingers. She was twisting and turning as she gripped the sheets even harder. "OH FUCK!" "Aww, awww, awww," she said as her body quivered as she had a massive climax. Her body dropped back onto the bed, Eric was now satisfied that he had just given her one of the best orgasms of her life, and he could actually feel her pussy vibrating. She looked at him, he could see her trying to hold back the tears, but they still came out of her eyes. She got up and then said, "now, you lay down, baby, and let me took care of you, please."

Eric laid down on the bed as she instructed and watched as she slowly hovered over him. She slowly took his long, hard dick in her mouth. As Karen looked at Eric's dick, it was a beautiful, golden brown with small black veins running along it. She took this beautiful hard dick and began sucking it. She sucked onto his dick slowly at first, and then increased her momentum; she sucked it as if she were sucking a lollipop. She stopped and looks up at him, and said, "You like that, you like my mouth on that big dick, don't you?" Eric was caught up in the moment that he could barely got a response out, he simply replied, "Uh huh." She could hear him moaning while she was sucking his dick and she knew he was enjoying every minute of it. She put her mouth around the entire dick and with one hard suck, she began sucking his cock.

Her mouth went crazy over his dick, first sucking it long and hard, and then slowing down a little, and then picking up the pace again. This time, sucking his dick then licking it and then kissing it and licking it again. It was driving him crazy, but she could see him, fighting his feelings trying to keep it together. Although she would love to continue sucking his dick until she could taste his juices inside her mouth, she knew that he would die if he did not got to fuck her tonight. She looked up at him and said, "You wanna fuck this little pussy, don't you?"

Eric looked at her with a smile on his face and replied, "Hell, yeah."

She knew that he loved hitting it from behind, and although this was not her favorite position, she was willing to let him had his way tonight.

"Tell me what you wanna do, you wanna hit it from the back, baby?" she asked him. She did not had to ask twice, he sprung off the bed and instructed her to come bend over on the bed in front him, so he could fuck her from behind. Karen did as she was told and before she could breathe, she felt his hot dick rubbing against her pussy from the back. He forced his dick inside her pussy, and soon his dick was ramming inside her pussy. He gripped her by her butt cheeks and used that as support as he launched his massive cock inside her with several mighty thrusts. Karen enjoyed this rough sex and she moaned as he fucked her and shrieked, "Oh my God, yeah, yeah, umm... oh, yes!" Her groaned escaped her lips as she was fucked by her new husband.

His movements intensify, and he grabbed her ass tighter, spanking her and yelling, "Hell yeah! Oh yeah, baby! This was good pussy!" Then, with one huge thrust that almost threw her over the bed, he exploded inside her pussy. His hot cum was gushing outside her pussy as he pulled away.

They both collapsed on the bed together, from exhaustion and fell asleep in each other's arms.

"Wow, this place looks amazing!" Marcia said, as they stepped out of the taxi. They were now in Saint Lucia standing in front of the Sandals Grande Resort, the hotel where they would be staying while on the island. The hotel itself was huge and it had a certain degree of elegance in the architectural design. They were met by one of the hotel staff members with cocktails and moist towels. It was about three thirty in the afternoon when they got to the hotel. They proceeded to the front desk to check in. "Mr and Mrs Grey, please," Danny told the young lady behind the reception counter. She was dressed in a bright blue suit with a pink scarf. As they made their way to their room, they were greeted on their way there by all the staff members that passed by. Everyone here seemed to be really pleasant.

Their room was beautifully decorated and

rose petals were used on the bed to write a welcome message which read, "Congratulations on your 16th Anniversary." Marcia remembered telling the reservation agent on the phone that they would be celebrating their wedding anniversary the day before, but she did not expect them to remember that, much less remember how many years they were celebrating. Therefore, she was impressed to know that the hotel probably did really care about their guests. Their room was filled with brochures of Saint Lucia and Danny noticed that there was a bottle of red wine on the night stand with a box of chocolates next to it.

"Wow, seems like they went all out," he said laughing. Marcia was happy to see her husband smiling and laughing again. The past few months had been really hard on them, they had been having lots of arguments. Most of the arguments that they were having stemmed from the same issue, the twenty three year old secretary named Evelyn that Danny had hired about a year ago. However, this was not the time to think about any of that. After all, they were thousands of miles away from work and Evelyn.

Marcia had their vacation planned out; she had an agenda; which included a tour of the southern part of the island, coulddle-light dinners, scuba diving, a historical tour and much more. After getting settled into their room, they went to the bar for drinks before going to dinner at one of the hotel's most exquisite restaurants. While at the bar, they met other couples on vacation and engaged in lively conversations about the hotel and the island in general.

They found out that Saint Lucia was also called the Helen of the West, because both the French and the English fought over the island. In fact, the two nations had a fourteen year battle over the island in an effort to colonize it and make money off of producing and selling sugar from there. They also found out that there were three Sandals Resorts on the island; however, Sandals Grande, which they were staying at, was the largest and most elegant of the three. The spent almost the entire evening at the bar, drinking and laughing then they decided to put off the dinner for the following evening, they ordered burgers and French fries and went back to their rooms.

Since they had stayed up late last night having fun, Marcia decided to do something romantic and put in a special request for breakfast in bed for her and her husband. The doorbell rang, and a young man with an island accent could be heard saying, "Room service."

Marcia went to got the door and the young man rolled a cart inside the room, he had several plates on this cart and as he uncovered them, a sweet aroma filled the room. It was her favorite: homemade waffles and chicken strips. There was also a jug of fresh squeezed orange juice, some muffins in a basket, milk, two miniature-sized boxes of cereal and two fruit plates, with slices of cantaloupe, watermelon, strawberries, banana and grapes. It looked amazing, she asked the butler to place the food on the table in their small porch area for their suite, and then went in to wake her husband up. "Happy Anniversary, my love," she whispered as she gently nibbled on his ears.

Although Dan was awake, he had chosen to keep his eyes closed and enjoy what little affection his wife was giving to him right now. For some time now, she had been consumed with her job and helping the children there. She had gotten so involved, she began talking about having children, and although Dan did not mind having one child, having more than one would be a problem. Dan had always been an only child and he enjoyed so many privileges that his classmates never got; therefore he always believed that having one child was best.

As she nibbled on his eyes, he remembered how playful she used to be before getting what he referred to as "her baby fever."

Dan finally opened his eyes laughing. "Okay, okay, I'm up," he told her. Marcia could tell after a while that he was just pretending to be sleeping, but still continued nibbling on his ears.

Dan got out of the bed and they went to the patio where they enjoyed a lovely breakfast while taking in the beautiful view of the beach. When they finished breakfast, Marcia went into the shower, and invited her husband to join her there.

During recent times, they barely touched each other and Marcia was determined to change that. She wanted her husband back, she wanted to save her marriage, but most importantly, she wanted to start raising a family. She was already naked under the water, and as Dan walked in he could see the profile of her perfect figure through the glass door in the shower. Although she was in her late thirties, she had the body of a twenty year old.

She looked tall and slender and as he opened the door, she turned around to watch him. His dick instantaneously stood at attention. He realized that he had not seen his wife naked in what seemed like ages.

"Gosh, you look, beautiful," he said to her and he hurriedly removed his boxer shorts. She looked down at his erect dick and from the look on her face; he could tell that she was pleased. He looked at her intensely with water dripping off her skin, her hair was tucked away in a ponytail which he reached out and removed, releasing her long beautiful brown hair. Dan looked at his wife from her head to her feet, carefully measuring every each of her body, and at that moment, he regretted every wrong thing he ever did to her. He had a beautiful wife at home who loved him, who wanted to had children and grow old with him, and he treated her like she was the enemy.

Dan moved in closer to his wife and planted a soft, gentle kiss of her lips. Almost suddenly, she grabbed hold of his lips with hers and passionately kissed him. Her kiss was long and hard, filled with yearning and desire. This was all Dan needed; he had not been sure how this shower would go, but now he knew that she wanted him. He began kissing her back, and as their bodies touched together, they both moaned out loud. The fire between them had been ignited.

"I missed you," Marcia whispered in his ear.

"I love you, Marcia Grey," he replied as he began slowly running his tongue down along the nape of her neck and down to her tiny round nipples. She could feel the sensations - they were unlike anything she felt before. She moaned with pleasure, as the water trickled down her back. His tongue continued exploring her body, gliding slowly down to the core of her womanhood. When he got to her pussy, he got down on his knees and looked at it, then looked up at her with a smile on his face.

Her pussy was small with a line of brownish hair running down the middle, the flesh itself looked untouched. He knew that she had definitely not been cheating on him. He parted her legs leaving one on the floor while placing her other leg on the small stool in the shower. Marcia could hardly wait for what was coming next as he stroked her pussy with his fingers.

A loud moan escapes her lips as she felt his tongue run wild over her inner pussy. As Dan tried to took the entire pussy in his mouth, he almost loses himself in the moment, and began to lick her pussy harder. He licked her clitoris hard and then moved to licking her pussy lips. Then he moved his tongue further down and flicked his tongue back and forth up and down her tiny pink slit. He then stuck it into the pussy whole itself, and fucked her pussy with his tongue, pushing his face upwards as he explored her insides with his tongue.

"Aww, yes, baby," Marcia moaned as she could feel her juices running down her body like electricity. He continued to suck her pussy and she could feel his dick throbbing as she moaned and quivered to the feel of his tongue in her pussy. He pulled out before she could climax and rubbed his hand all over his dick, motioning her to got down on her knees and suck it.

Marcia went down on her knees and took Dan's dick in her mouth, sucking it hard. She slowly pulled the dick out of her mouth and passed her tongue gently around the head of his dick. Then she flicked her tongue back and forth on the head, licking it head slowly.

Dan definitely loved the moment and his body began to tremble. She pulled back slowly and delicately, reached for his balls and gently massages them as she tightened her grip on his dick with her sucking.

"Oh, God," Dan moaned and tried to took a deep breath to control himself.

"Hmmm," she said as she nibbled her tongue on his dick.

"Ooooooooooooooohh," Dan groaned as he enjoyed the sensations that his wife was bringing about with her tongue. He could feel that he might cum any minute, but he knew that he wanted to fuck her first. So he pulled her head off his dick and said, "I want that pussy baby, I want it soo bad." Marcia stood up and began kissing him hard; he, too, kissed her passionately. He gripped her ass and pushed her up against the shower walls and right there, he began to fuck her hard. They were standing up and she had one of her legs wrapped around him as he stuck his dick inside her. He could feel the tightness of her pussy and he was enjoying the moaned that she made every time he thrust inside her. As she fucked her, he began to kiss her neck; that drove her wild and she moaned even more. Her pussy felt like it was a vibrator, and the walls were contracting around his. He couldn't help it when "baby" slips out. She was blowing his mind away with all of this. He began to increase his momentum and gripped her ass even harder as he lost himself inside her pussy.

"Oh God, baby," she moaned back. Their bodies now act like one, and they had rhythmic movements.

They were now both moaning together and the pleasure was intense. "Oh God, yes, yes!" She moaned as she felt she was at the brink of her climax.

"I'm gonna cum, Oh, shit," Dan said as he further rammed his dick inside her pussy even harder. "Oh, Oh, Oh, shit!" He shouted as he exploded with cum all inside her. She too, climaxed with him and could feel his hot cum gushing out of her pussy. They both try to calm down and hold each other while trying to catch their breath.

"I love you," she said to her husband and

kissed him. Then she put her head on his chest as he stood under the shower. "I love you too, sweetheart," he replied as he planted a kiss on her forehead. They remained in the shower as they soap each other's bodies and took turns under the water. When they got out of the shower, they decided to relax on their porch for a minute before heading out around town.

The rest of their day was spent on shopping and eating out. They purchased souvenirs from a local craft market to take back home. One of the souvenirs that they purchased was a small bird house made from a dried coconut.

They had lunch at a waterfront restaurant called "The Coal Pot." They enjoyed one of the local meals of "Green Figs and Salt Fish" made with ingredients such as green bananas and salted cod fish with a side of steamed vegetables. When it was about five in the evening, they headed back to the hotel to got ready for a romantic dinner that Marcia had reserved at one of the best restaurants at the hotel.

Eric had had a good day. He had spent it fishing with his new wife, and fishing had been something she loved doing, so he had used this opportunity to took her fishing and whale watching together. He had to admit, he had thought married life would be different, but when he got up after a great night, he felt bored. There he was on this beautiful island, and he was bored. Was it due to the fact that his new wife was such a mild and timid person, an introvert, while he, was a wild, vibrant, extrovert?

His best friend Ben had told him of his disapproval of this entire wedding. He could hear Ben's voice clearly in his ears. "Eric, bro, don't mean to be your party poppa or anything, but I know you man, and she ain't the one... you guys were so different."

At that time, Eric thought this would had been a good thing. After all, he did not want to be with someone who was exactly like him. However, the truth was starting to sink in, they did not had any similarities, it seemed like anything she likes, he dislikes. took for example this little fishing trip; he hated fishing, he did not like whale watching either. These were two of the most boring things a guy could do right along the line of shopping, which Karen had conveniently scheduled for the next day.

He had decided that he was not having any more of this girly stuff; he wanted to go scuba diving and wind surfing. Basically, he wanted an island adventure, and shopping, fishing and whale watching did not fall into this category. However, as he looked at her face, it was filled with excitement and he could see her taking photos of the whales they had spotted, he forced himself to endure what seemed like an entire day but was actually a few hours of fishing and whale watching.

"Damn, I must, really love this girl," he thought to himself, as he sat down trying to enjoy the only thing he liked on this trip: a cold beer.

When they got back to their rooms, he wanted to had sex but she said that if they do it too much, they might not got to really enjoy what they island had to offer. "We're here, let's enjoy the ambiance, and we could make love anytime," she said with a smile on her face.

He could see that she was really into something much deeper than sex. "For crying out loud, we were on our honeymoon, wasn't that where we were supposed to make love?" he thought to himself.

However, he did not reveal his thoughts to her for fear that it might start an argument. They decided to spend the rest of the day exploring the hotel by checking out the restaurants and bars, the gift shop and doing a photo shoot together.

By the time night came, Eric was drained from doing that kind of stuff, not to mention the lack of sex for that day. He just wanted to drink some red wine, make love to his wife and go to bed.

But of course this was not what Karen had planned. She wanted them to take tonight and work on building their spiritual connection. She believed that if they had a deeper connection, something more than just sex and love making, then that would make their marriage stronger. "If we could lay next to each other naked and simply admire each other, and look into each other's eyes and try to envision our future together, just imagine how strong our relationship would be, baby," she told him, as she kissed him softly.

"Okay, but I need a drink. Let me run to the bar real quick," he quickly exited the room before she could stop him and made his way to the bar, where he did not had one drink. In fact, he had several drinks. He could not believe her nerve. He had just spent the entire day doing stuff that she liked. It was beginning to seem like she was the only one on her honeymoon because this was definitely not his idea of a great honeymoon vacation. "Another Bacardi, straight up" Eric said as he motioned for another drink from the bartender.

As seven o'clock approached, Marcia quickly put on her earrings. She was wearing one of the new outfits that she bought especially for this trip. It was a red figure hugging tube dress a few inches above her knees, with lace trimmings along the edges. When Dan had gotten out of the shower and saw her all dressed up, he looked at her like a lion ready to pounce on its prey. It was clear that he was mesmerized with her and he wanted her.

"You look amazing," he said and gave her a kiss on her hand.

"Thanks, but hurry, you need to got dressed. Dinner starts at seven," she replied. Every time they had to go out, she would always be the first to got ready; Dan could never got ready quickly enough. He would took what seemed like hours shaving and brushing his hair, and then he would took his shower. She just did not understand why it took so long for him to got ready to go out, however if it were work related, he would be out of the house in a few minutes. They finally head to dinner at about half past seven, in their most elegant evening attire.

The Greys headed down to the pier, where Gordon's Restaurant was located. It was the most exquisite restaurant at the hotel. They were greeted at the door by the hostess and soon they were seated. As Dan looked at his wife, he could see a glow on her face. She seemed really happy to be here. She smiled at him, and then looked at her menu.

Their night was perfect so far. Marcia could not ask for anything more, but all of sudden Dan's cell phone was vibrating. Someone was calling him; he pulled out the cell phone from his pocket and looked down at it under the table. Marcia looked at him, and she watched as facial expression changed to one of irritation that someone would call him at nine in the night, to what seemed like a smile and his face lit up.

Right in the moment a gut feeling told her that it could be Evelyn, but she wanted to be wrong, so she waited to see what he would say.

"I need to took this honey," he said and got up from his seat and used the nearest exit. After what seemed like almost an hour Marcia went out to see why her husband was still not back. She saw him seated outside on the wall in front of the restaurant. He was still on his phone; however he had gotten comfortable and had his tie loosened. He seemed to had completely forgotten that she was inside waiting for him to return.

Marcia was concerned - could it be an emergency at work? She walked up to him, and whispered, "what's wrong honey, work?"

He simply brushed her off, and whispered back to her, "Oh no, it's just Ev, she wanted to go over some stuff with me." Marcia could hardly believe her ears, her eyes almost popped out of its sockets, and like a volcano she exploded and threw a tantrum outside the restaurant.

She grabbed the phone from him and flings it across into some bushes.

"How dare you!" Dan shouts in the angriest voice she had ever heard. "You must had lost your goddamn mind!" he continued.

Before he continued, she cut him short with her crying, "How could you? How could you do this to us, to me?" Marcia said.

"Do what?" he replied angrily, "Listen, I am not making a scene out here with your ass in front of this place." He left her there and walked away very upset. Marcia went after him, and followed him to their room. When she got into the room, she continued with her rants at him.

"You're all the way in Saint Lucia; I don't understand why you two need to speak to each other. She's not your WIFE, Danny!" Marcia shrieked.

Their marriage had had its ups and downs, but the situation got worse when Danny hired a twenty-three year old secretary named

Evelyn.

Danny and his secretary would spend hours on the phone every day, they went to dinners together, he would go to some of her family events, and she would attend his. Marcia could not believe that the only time she got with her husband without any disruption was being interrupted, by Evelyn, of course.

Finally, Marcia mustered all her courage to ask what had been on her mind for six months now, "Did you do it?" He looked at her and from the look in his eyes she knew the answer to her question; however, he still pretended like he did not know what she was insinuating.

"Do what?" he replied.

"Did you fuck her, Dan? I'm not stupid. The phone calls, the evenings out, did you fuck Evelyn? Please tell me the truth, I couldnot live this lie. Just be honest for once, please?" She was crying so much that she could barely breathe, her face was red, and she had tears running down her cheeks.

When she heard the answer to her question, it felt like someone had plunged a dagger into her heart. For months she wanted to know the truth, but here she was wishing she never asked. "How could you, how could you?" She shouted at him. He was moving closer to her, to try to embrace her, but she was not having it; as he moved closer, she moved backwards.

"I trusted you while you were sleeping with your secretary. I hate you. We were done, you hear me? DONE!" she shouted angrily and stormed out of the room.

Although he wanted to run after her and kiss her, and try to get her to forgive him, Dan knew that she would only push him away further.

He had never intended to cheat on his wife, or hurt her. When he met Evelyn, it was strictly business. She was young and attractive, and she would create a good image for him with his colleagues. It never crossed his mind that he would one day cheat on his wife with her. How it happened, he did not even remember; he just recalled that after some time he used her as his comfort whenever he had problems with his wife. Soon they were in a relationship and they were going out to functions and dinners, and evening going on short rendezvous together.

He never wanted his wife to find out, especially not like this on their vacation that she had been planning for years. He began to regret even hiring Evelyn in the first place, he should have known better. The look on his wife's face when she heard the news broke his heart. He never wanted to hurt her again. He wanted his wife back, and he would do anything to get her back, anything.

As he sat on his bed lonely and full of regret and disgust with himself, he could not fight back the tears. He cried profusely, he had never cried like this before, except when he lost his dad. How could he do that to a woman who loved him so much, who would do anything for him, who would never cheat on him? He was a horrible person.

As Marcia stormed out of the room, she needed to be alone. She could not stand the sight of his lying, cheating face. She walked around crying for a bit, thinking about all the signs she had been seeing. She finally decided that if it would jeopardize his marriage for sex with a little girl, she would let him go so he could enjoy all the baggage that came with it.

As soon as she got home, the first thing she would be doing was calling a divorce lawyer. She had given this man the best years of her life, and yet he did not care, he just kept hurting her over and over.

In a few minutes Marcia went from being sad and hopeless to being depressed to being upset. Ultimately she wanted revenge. She wanted him to feel the pain she had felt, she wanted to leave her life carefree while he suffered and paid for his mistakes. She went to the bar and got a drink then headed to the pool. There was no one in sight and soon, the feeling of loneliness and sadness crept in upon her again. She couldn't help but cry her eyes out.

Her tears were cut short when she realized that the water was moving and possibly there could be someone in the water. Just when she was about to leave the pool side and head to the bar, she saw this beautiful man emerge out of the pool. She thought she was dreaming. He was not handsome, he was beautiful, God's perfect creation. His body was dripping wet, and the droplets of water were glimmering on his skin; chocolate brown in complexion, his lips were cherry pink. He was by far the sexiest bald-headed guy she had ever seen. He had a huge tiger tattoo on his left arm and he was definitely athletic, his six-pack was one of the most attractive things on his body. He was walking towards, and he could feel her eyes moving all over him like a laser beam. Marcia looks at him with lust in her eyes and sensations rushing within. She watched his beautiful six pack abs and ran her star downward to the perfect V-shape of his muscles leading down to his wet trunks. She wondered what was in those pants. He walked straight up to her, and in the most sexy-gruff voice she had ever heard asked, "Why were you sitting here crying, beautiful?"

At that moment, for the first time in her life, Marcia completely forgot about the drama going on and decided to do something wild and exciting. "I am not crying," she replied, trying to fake a tiny smile, as she wiped the tears off her cheek.

Eric had just gone for a swim after a few drinks in the bar and when he suspected that he was not alone, he came out of the water. There in the middle of the night was a gorgeous black woman crying. In the past he used to be a heart breaker, and he had seen more than his fair share of "crocodile tears" as her referred to them. However, this woman's tears seemed sincere and he really wanted to know what was wrong. After all, no one as beautiful as she was should be crying. He sat next to her, and they introduced themselves and began talking. She maintained that she was going to be okay and never got to the main reason why she was crying. The only thing he got out from her was that someone had spoiled her night. Their conversation soon branched out into talking about sports, then talking about the island and how beautiful it was. He mentioned that he had wanted to go on a tour of the island, most probably to the southern part, since that was where most of the island's attractions were.

They were soon getting really comfortable with each other, and as she got up to leave, their heads met and like electricity, the attraction between them was immense. He kissed her and then she kissed him back, and they both went wild in each other's mouths. Their kisses were wild and they were ravishing each other outside in the middle of the night in front of the pool. They decided to stop before they were seen and moved to the secluded area, in the gym by the pool.

They closed the door in the back and proceeded to pick up where they left off. Her lips were filled with desire, he had never been the type of guy to turn down an attractive woman, and he was definitely not going to start tonight. He ran his fingers down her back until he got to her butt. It was a cute, tiny round butt, just the type that he normally went for. As he kissed her, he felt her hand going down into his trunks searching. When she found his dick she gripped onto it tightly and started to caress it with her hands.

Marcia wanted this man bad, she had never felt anything like this, more so far a total stranger. When she felt his big hard dick, she instantly wanted to taste it.

She whipped out his dick and began to suck on it. She licked it, like she was licking an ice-cream or a lollipop. His dick was enormous; slightly bent at the head, and talking about his head, it was huge. She caressed the head of his dick with her tongue and he moaned with pleasure. He pulled her up off of her knees where she had been sucking his dick and laid her on her back on the floor. He quickly climbs on top her and used his dick to find her pussy hole. As he gradually entered her, she moaned even more. When he was inside her, he could fill that she was completely wet with desire and the inside of her pussy was hotter than the rest of her body. He began thrusting his dick inside her with slowly long strokes at first. She gripped on to his arm and moaned a loud "ooooooooooohh," as if she were singing a song. She was gently biting and kissing on his neck as he entered her repeatedly. The excitement built up, and the more he thrust insides her, the more he felt like he was about to lose himself.

"This had to be the best pussy I've ever had," he thought to himself. His thrust increases in momentum, but now, he did not pull out of her pussy as much. He was deep down inside of her and he was now just ramming his dick in her. She braced in his arms, and had her legs up wrapped around his waist area. He continued to go deeper and deeper within her, the thrust were harder and harder, and he finally explodes inside her sweet pussy. Marcia had also been enjoying the moment and she also climaxes with him. Their bodies were now exhausted as they try to catch their breath.

"What had just happened?" Marcia thought to herself. Eric kissed her on her forehead and got up out of her, trying to use his shorts to whip off the cum on his dick. "Wow, you were amazing," he said to her.

"You were pretty good too, yourself," she replied, as she stood up, trying to pull herself together. She did not even remember when or how she took off her red dress; she just saw it in a corner together with her panties. The panties were torn up; he must have ripped them off to get to her pussy.

This was just all so fast, she just went with her feelings and in doing so, had one of the wildest, most pleasurable moments of her life. Marcia was more satisfied with these few minutes of passion than she had ever been with the sixteen years of sex she had been having with her husband. When they were done getting dressed, they kissed each other and went their separate ways. That night when Eric got to his room, he was happy his wife was fast asleep; he took a quick shower and sat on the couch wondering why he had just cheated on his wife with this mysterious stranger while on his honeymoon.

As Marcia walked back to her room, she had to admit that she did feel a sense of guilty pleasure. She had just cheated on her husband with a stranger, and he had deserved every bit of it. This vacation may not be so bad after all. She would just do everything that he ever did to her; they were going to be divorced anyway, so she did not care.

When she got to the room, Danny was still up waiting for her with a worried look on his face. "Where were you? Look, Marcia, I'm really sorry. I never meant for any of this to happen. I know you're mad, and you probably hate me, but please, believe me. I love you baby, and I want only you, I don't care about Evelyn, she meant nothing to me," he said.

She looked at him, and she could see that his eyes were swollen from crying. She did love him, but she could not forgive him. She just walked straight passed him and replied coldly, "I'm tired, goodnight."

"He could stay up thinking about how much he hurt me," she thought to herself, and turned her back on him.

Marcia woke up the following morning to the sound of Dan's voice. He was gently nibbling on her ears. She pulled away and asks him to stop it. Clearly, she was irritated at him. He had ordered room service and he asked her to join him for breakfast on the porch. Marcia was not feeling up to it; her thoughts were consumed with the events of the previous night. In particular, she remembered how she felt, when she was laying down on the floor of the gym while Eric was thrusting his massive cock inside her pussy. Just the thought of Eric brought a smile to her face. He was definitely younger than her. He looked like he was probably in his mid-twenties, while she was in her later thirties. "That's so crazy," she thought to herself, feeling somewhat like a cougar.

Today, she had planned to go on a tour of the island with her husband, but because of everything that happened last night, she was definitely not feeling up to do anything like that. She actually wanted to just sleep in today; she could tell that she would probably be in a deep depression the entire day.

She knew that Dan was probably feeling horrible, and he should. He had cheated on her and was bold enough to admit it. Even with everything that happened last night, although upset and hurt at the time, she felt a little bad now.

Eric woke up and saw his wife on the bed; he had fallen asleep on the couch. He walked over to the bed. She was still asleep; he planted a soft kiss on her forehead. He never wanted her to find out what he had done last night. He felt like he had done the ultimate betrayal, he had cheated on his wife on their honeymoon. However, he could not stop thinking about this other woman, what had attracted him to her, was it that he pitied her because she was clearly hurting? He got into the bed and lay down holding his wife.

Today, he actually just wanted to hold her, and he felt horrible. Her back was turned towards him; he moved in closer and wrapped his hand around her waist. She must have felt his body next to hers because she slid closer to him and got more comfortable.

They both got out of bed when it's about ten in the morning. Eric decided that he wanted to do something special for his wife. He calls the front desk and schedules a fun afternoon at Rain Forest Sky Rides. Rain Forest Sky Rides was a nature reserve in Saint Lucia where you could zip line through the rainforest. However, when they got to the rainforest, Karen got cold feet and as they were about to get strapped onto the zip line, Karen decided to let Eric go for the ride by himself.

Eric was furious, he really wanted her to do something that he enjoyed doing. Eric began thinking about Marcia; when she was aroused she was so full of life. He was sure that if she were the one here with him, she would be on that zip line having fun. He began yearning to be with her, and even though he regretted cheating on his wife, he now believed that if he ever saw Marcia, he would probably cheat again.

Since they were at a couples resort, he knew that she was not alone. Was she there with her boyfriend, or even worse, was she there with her husband? He did not know. He never asked her who she was with or what day she was leaving, there was so little that he knew about her. He did not just want to see her; he needed to see her again.

When they left the rain forest sky rides, they headed straight to their rooms to freshen up and got ready for a night out in the town. Along their way back, Karen kept apologizing to him, and mentioned that she was terrified of great heights. "Why didn't you tell me that?" Eric said in a tone of frustration. If he had known he would have never even taken here there.

"It's okay," he said just to shut her up but it really bothered him. Karen went to take her shower first while Eric sat watching TV. A few minutes later, she came out wearing nothing but her earrings, and she proceeded to seduce him. However, it was too late, he was not interested, and he was consumed with the desire to see Marcia Grey again. He sprung from his seat when he realized what she was doing, and made comments about how he was tired and needed a hot shower. When he got out of the shower, he got dressed and left the room. Before leaving, he told her he was going to find out what activities they had at the resort, then he would come back to the room in a while to took her to dinner. Karen, realizing that he was still upset, allowed him to leave hoping that he would soon get over his anger towards her.

He walked around the hotel with one thing on his mind, finding Marcia. He looked everywhere, by the pool, in the bars, in the restaurants that were opened, in the gym, in the gift shop, but she was nowhere to be found.

Finally, he went to reception, and tipped one of the guys there in exchange for the extension number for the room. He then slipped into the bar and asked for a quick call to his room, the bartender allowed him to call his room. As he dialed Marcia Grey's room number, he had his fingers crossed hoping that her husband did not answer the phone. He would just hang up if heard a male's voice on the other end of the call.

He was so relieved when she picked up the phone. "Hello," she said.

"Hi, Marcia, this was Eric from last night, I was wondering if we could we meet up sometime tonight?" he asked, not knowing what her reply would be.

"Umm, yeah, sure," she replied. They then spoke briefly about their day. He had set up a date with her for tonight at the gym, at eleven in the night. His face lit up as he looked forward to his date with her. That night after dinner, Eric faked a headache, and said that he was so tired that he needed a rest. By the time it was about a quarter to eleven, his wife was fast asleep; he silently crept out of the bed and makes his way to the gym to meet Marcia.

When Marcia got to the gym, she waited for Eric and when he arrived, they decide to go to the beach for a nice romantic walk. As they walk along the shore, they recap what how they spent their day. Marcia opens up to Eric and told him about her husband, and how he cheated on her with his secretary. She told Eric everything. He held her hands, and assures her that things were going to get better for her.

He then shared some of the problems that he had been having with his with her. Marcia was like a breath of fresh air; she did not judge she simply smiles and told him to not worry too much about what he was going through now. They stopped next to a wall and continued talking. After a while, he moved in closer to her, and pressing her back against the wall, he kissed her passionately. As they continued kissing, she gently ran her hands down his crotch and unzipped the zipper of his khaki shorts. Her hand explored the insides of his shorts and then pulled out his dick as she went down on her knees. He changed positions with her, and now his back was up against the wall, with his legs slightly opened, and his penis erect.

Marcia gently cupped his dick with both hands and began to lick it vigorously, up and down, side to side; she pulled her head back briefly and said, "It tastes so good."

She continued sucking his dick as if it were a lollipop. All the while, she was feeling an awesome sensation between her legs she began sucking it harder this time. He pushes his penis deep into her mouth, causing her to gag. He then pulled out a little and pushes it back in. His dick was huge and it filled up her entire mouth. He began to shove this dick harder as if he were trying to get her to swallow it. She pulled back and took a deep breath, and continued sucking his dick this time giving it long strokes with her tongue. After a while, his dick was heavily covered with her saliva and his precum. Marcia positioned her head under the dick, and sucked his dick from that angle. It was driving him crazy; he pulled out his penis from her mouth. Marcia still wanted to suck his dick some more but he stopped her. "Let me see that sexy body," he said to her and helped her stand up.

Eric's eyes were glued on to her and he watched intensely as she took her clothes off. She was wearing a short, white summer dress. Underneath the dress, she had a sexy black lace bra and a thong. As she unstrapped her bra, her breasts bounced out of it, and they looked big and full. Her nipples were hard and round and he could tell that she was aroused. He grabbed her closer to him, and rips out the thong with one strong pull. They both smile as they look into each other's eyes completely naked and filled with desire. He kissed her gently and used his hand to cup her head; he kissed her some more and lays her down on the sand, then he gently caressed her breasts with his tongue. He used his hands to spread her legs wide open, his fingers probe the opening between her legs. It was wet and he knew she needed to have his dick inside her pussy. As he brushed his fingers gently all over her pussy, a few moans escaped her lips. She was ready to receive him. "You naughty girl," he said to her, "you're dripping wet."

"I've never been so horny," she giggled nervously. Eric proceeded to explore her pussy some more, this time with his tongue. He gently glides his tongue along the insides of her pussy, and then he flicked his tongue back and forth, on her clitoris.

"Ooooooooooohh... this felt so good," she moaned with pleasure. He increased the pace of his licking while using his hands to gently squeeze her tits.

"Oh, God!" she shrieked as she felt the sensations run wild through her body. Before she could cum, he stopped and moved on top of her. He kissed her some more and sticks his dick deep down inside her pussy. He was thrusting his dick faster and faster inside her pussy while kissing her hard. He then rolls over, and now she finds herself seated on his dick. She began riding his dick, up and down, and then harder and faster. He gripped her ass the way a biker held on to the handles of his bike. He was slamming her pussy on his dick and enjoying every minute of him.

Marcia was now riding him harder and moaning loudly. This had to be the best sex she had ever had. He breasts were bouncing up and down, and her waist making movements that she never even thought were possible. She could feel that she was about to cum, she braced her hand on his shoulders, closed her eyes and lost herself in the ecstasy of the moment.

Danny was very worried about Marcia; she just got up out of bed at almost eleven and said she needed to go out for fresh air and a drink. He knew that he hurt her really bad, and he was trying to not be too pushy. He knew that she had stayed in bed the entire day, she had barely eaten anything. He was so sorry for putting her through all the bad stuff.

He looked at his phone; he had twenty missed calls from Evelyn in one night. He needed to put an end to this, she had destroyed his marriage, and he did not even really love her. Although he cared about her and wanted to see her doing well in her career and in life, he did not see himself having a life with her. The sex with her was great; she never nagged him about anything until recently. She was becoming irritatingly clingy. She was always calling him about some urgent issue which was always never really urgent in reality.

Tonight he missed his wife terribly and here the enemy was, "blowing up his phone." He finally answered his phone and in a firm affirmative voice he told her that it was over. He told her that he had told his wife, and she was completely devastated over the entire thing. He also told her that when he returned to work, they would need to work out the terms of her employment and he would decide whether he would have her transferred to work with someone else.

Evelyn was not at all happy about this; she swore at him, and called him all sorts of names. In the end, she told him that he would come back to her. He hung up the phone and waited for his wife. He wanted to inform her that he had ended things with his mistress and that he would not be working with her again. He also booked a tour for them to go on the following day, hoping that she would go with him and got out of her funk.

He fell asleep waiting for her to get back. The following morning, however, he got up early and ordered room service again for breakfast. He had all her favorite. When he got up brought the breakfast tray over to her side of the bed, and rang a little bell to wake her up. Marcia woke up and saw her husband seated on her side of the bed with a breakfast tray on his lap.

She was surprised he was really trying to go all out to impress her. "Please eat something, Marcia," he begged her. "I love you and its killing me to see you like this," he continued.

She sat up and greeted him, and for the first time since the night of his confession, she spoke to him, and she was actually smiling. She had not forgiven him but she could try to be cordial. They had a beautiful breakfast. Then he told her about the tour of the southern part of the island that he had booked for them. She decided that it would not hurt to go, so she got up took a shower and soon they were ready to leave.

They headed out on their tour and along the way to the south, they spoke with the locals, and touched a huge boa constrictor snake named Nick. On the south of this island, seated in front of the ocean were two majestic twin peaks, and it was said that the sun sets and rises in the crest of the two mountains, making them an absolute beauty to see.

They had fresh grilled fish, right on the beach, for lunch. They took several pictures together, and they had a great day. They ended their day with a romantic dinner specially prepared by the island's top gourmet chef.

After dinner, Marcia and her husband headed back to her room. Dan was determined to win her back. He had a gift for her, he handed her a small black box. She opened it and to her surprise it had the most beautiful diamond ring in it. It must have cost him a fortune; it had a huge diamond on top it. "Will you marry me again, Marcia Jerkins?" he asked as he got down on his knees.

Marcia could not believe this, she had not seen this coming, and he must have really been feeling bad, because he usually never bought her diamonds. She was at a loss for words. In all honesty she did love her husband, but he had really hurt her. "Can you give me some time to think about it?" she said, as she ran out of the room.

Marcia went to the pool and sat there, trying to put things in perspective and deciding what she would do. She keeps thinking about Eric, she realizes that she had done almost the same thing with her husband. When things had gotten bad, she ran to someone else for comfort. How could she chastise him, when she herself had just cheated on him? Marcia knew that she did not love Eric, she loved her husband.

Evelyn was a mere fling, and now as he was on the vacation with her, and although he hurt her he was now trying to do right by her. Marcia felt bad; her husband realized his mistake and was desperately seeking her forgiveness. She needed to speak to Eric to end whatever it was that they had and try to work on her marriage with Dan.

Marcia returns to her room and accepts her husband's wedding proposal. "When were we making this happen?" She asked him.

"First thing tomorrow at nine," he replied, "I have already spoken to the wedding coordinator." He seemed to have everything planned out.

She smiled at him, and that night they made love like they did the first night they met. The following morning, they got up early and went to renew their vows at the hotel chapel. The rest of their day was spent in their hotel room making love and ordering room service.

Marcia, however, did need to speak with Eric to make sure that there were no hard feelings between them. She went to reception and left a message for him, and asks her to call her on her mobile phone. Eric was on his way to a scuba diving adventure he had booked, when the young woman at reception told him that she had a message for him. Instantly his mind clicked and he thought that it might be Marcia. When he saw the note, and the extension number it confirmed his thought.

Eric did not really know why Marcia wanted to speak with him. Had she fallen in love with him and wanted to confess her love for him.

He knew that it would be a sad thing if she had fallen for him, because he was surely not in love with her. In fact, he was still very much in love with his wife. He felt horrible; he knew his wife would die if she knew that.

She had sacrificed so much for him. Karen had moved to a whole new city just to be with him, and yet here he was disrespecting her while on their honeymoon. He needed to end this before it was too late but he knew it would be difficult for Marcia to deal with. After all, he too had felt these wild island sensations and did not want them to end. However when he took those vows he was making the decision to remain with his wife no matter what happened. He decided that he would tell Marcia tonight when they snuck out to see each other.

Marcia had spent the entire day romancing her husband in bed. When she met Eric that night she wanted to let him know that she had renewed her vows and that she would be leaving the island tomorrow. She was relieved when he said he wanted to end things.

As she left the rocks where they were seated on the beach, she decided that she would move forward and took what she had done to her grave. She did not intend to ever speak of this to her husband. Tomorrow, they would be checking out and flying back to Monroe, and these island sensations would be behind her. As she went back to her room that evening, her husband was up waiting for her. He asked where she had been. She made up some story about going out for some air to think about their relationship. She knew that he had changed.

A few weeks after they got back to Monroe, she was making breakfast when all of a sudden, she felt a little nauseous, and then she barely had time to make it to the bathroom before she began throwing up.

"You're pregnant," her husband told her, "I could tell, I feel sick, too," he had a smile on his face. She looked at him, and then realized that she did in fact put on some extra weight and she had been feeling nauseous recently and had been avoiding certain foods. Could she be pregnant at thirty eight?

Immediately, her husband went to the store to pick up a pregnancy test. When he got back they both went to the bathroom and stood there with their fingers crossed after she urinated on the little tip of the test. After their trip from the islands, her husband had changed for the better. He let his secretary go and he was at home more often. He would even cook for her some evenings, he had also mentioned that he did really want them to have at least one kid. When the three minutes had passed on his watch, Marcia picked up the test; there were two clear lines on there.

"Two lines babe," she told him, "it's positive." She could no longer hold back the tears. But this time, it was tears of joy. She had wanted to have his baby for over sixteen years and now it was finally going to happen.

He kissed her deeply and the test fell to the floor. He scooped her up in his arms, carried her to their bedroom, and her made sweet love to his pregnant wife. This was the beginning of a new chapter in Marcia's relationship and she did not know how it would turn out, but she knew that she was in a happy place with her husband.

Meanwhile in Co-op City, Eric and his new wife, Karen were adjusting well to married life. He was trying his hardest to take a new look at life from his wife's perspective. Although on the island it seemed that they had very few things in common, when they returned home, they began a massive home remodelling project on a new house that they purchased.

Eric was having fun renovating the house; breaking down the walls, and building the cupboards. He felt like a child all over again when he would pretend to be Bob the Builder, his favorite cartoon character growing up. Karen was having too much fun with the remodelling. She was doing the interior designing for the house. She enjoyed going shopping and picking out the drapery and other home décor. This house was the best thing that happened to the relationship, they were actually building their future together.

9 KELLY WILD-FIRE

As Ben looked across the aisle in the grocery store, he could see Kelly flirting with the guy stocking the shelves. He moved in closer to her, to hear exactly what was going on. She never even stopped to introduce him, all she said was, "You can go to the checkout, I'll be there in a minute."

It almost seemed like she was trying to run him off. How could any woman flirt with another guy while their boyfriend was standing right there? If someone had told him that he would be treated like that by the woman he loved, he would never have believed it.

Kelly Wildey, a.k.a Kelly 'Wild-fire,' had been the love of his life, and although many of his friends and family disliked her and her wild antics, there was something about her that Ben could not resist. She was a very attractive young woman, with a heavenly body, beautiful long hair, and a chocolate brown complexion. Her smile would light up the room, and she had a great sense of humor.

However, she loved partying and going out with her friends, and it was beginning to seem like she would never settle down and become the type of woman he would one day marry. Ben was a more serious laid back type of guy and he was older than Kelly, and a lot of the things that she now enjoyed, he had done in his younger days. He was now looking to settle down, get married and start a family.

How he wished he could do those things with Kelly but like her nickname, she went through life burning everything in her way, never settling down. One minute she was cool and calm, the next she was loud and rowdy, and the next she was in a state of, what he would call, 'high voltage,' and he just could not figure her out.

It had been over ten minutes since he checked out and paid for the stuff they had bought and yet Kelly was still nowhere to be seen.

"You can't be serious," he thought to himself as he stopped the engine and parked the car near the entrance of Wal-Mart. He pulled out his phone and dialled her number. After calling twice, she finally answered and was screaming at him.

"Where the hell were you!" she exclaims, "I been looking all over this damn place trying to find your ass!" she continued. After trying to calm her down, he let her know that he was at the entrance waiting for her. Eventually he saw her coming, her face was red with anger, and she entered the car, slams her door, and puts on her seat belt angrily. She looks at him, and said,

"So I can't talk to a friend anymore," she had failed to realize that he never had a problem with her talking to her friends, but what she did back there in the store was downright disrespectful.

When they got home, he had a headache, and just wanted to get as far away from her as he could. Lately he had been feeling that Kelly, and all her drama, were too much for him to handle. He didn't want to break up with her, but she was making it hard for him to stay. He took his car keys and went to get the groceries out of the trunk. After he put them on the kitchen counter, he took his keys and left.

"Where're you going?" she asked in that annoyingly rude tone of voice that he so hated.

He opened the door and walked out of the apartment. From outside in his car, he could hear loud talking in the front window. Did the drama ever end with this woman? He asked himself as he backed his car out into the road and drove away.

Kelly watched as he left, how could he be so cold towards her, but it was just like him. He always kept everything bottled up inside, and then he would just explode on her, days after, and she wouldn't even remember why he was upset.

Their relationship had been rocky ever since she had a miscarriage two years ago. She knew that he blames her for the loss of their child; she knew that he desperately wanted to be a father. Ben had so much love to give this child and it broke her heart when she heard the tragic news from her doctor.

"I'm sorry Kelly, but I can't find the baby's heartbeat," Dr. Anderson said to Kelly, one chilly summer afternoon. Kelly had been feeling ill the entire morning and when she started spotting, she had gone to see her doctor. The baby was only about twelve weeks along but they had bought almost everything they would need, from its diapers, to clothes, a crib, and even her stroller and car seat combo. Now what would had been the nursery was a room of broken dreams and painful memories. Kelly remembers the day they took the home pregnancy test; they were both so nervous and excited. They jumped with joy when they saw that the test was positive, they had even made love that night, and he had kissed her stomach and told the baby that everything would be okay. As these memories were coming back to her, Kelly's eyes were filled with tears, and she couldn't help but cry every time she remembered the unborn child that they lost.

It was probably about midnight when Ben finally returned home. Kelly was already asleep, and as he stepped into the room, he watched her as she slept peacefully in their bed. He would have laid down next to her but he just could not shake off the negative feeling that he felt towards her. He did not hate her, but he felt that she was the main reason for all the hurt that he felt. He had been in relationships before but he had never been with someone so much younger than him and who was not intimidated by him.

Kelly spoke her mind, and she did not care who was offended. As he continued to look at her, his feelings of anger turned into rage, and he wanted to teach her a lesson, and realized he was feeling a horny type of rage, he did not want to fight her or anything like that, he wanted to fuck her and get her to behave a little. He walked over to her side of the bed, and lifted the cover off of her. Her flesh was now exposed and he could see her in her most vulnerable state. She was wearing a white tank top and sexy pink panties. Her skin had a pretty natural glow, and as she slept there, he just enjoyed carefully examining her body with his eyes. He could not hold back any more.

He gently spread her legs open and pulled her panties to one side, he could now see her clean, shaved pussy. He wanted to taste it, as his tongue gently touched the inside of her pink pussy lips, her eyes popped open. She looked down at him, with sleep in her eyes, and watched as he removed her panties, she opened her legs wider allowing him access to the center of her womanhood.

Ben could feel his dick throbbing in his pants; she had given her approval by just the way she looked at him. He got up and stripped himself naked and then went back to pleasure her with his tongue. As he began to lick the insides of her pussy, she gradually began to come alive. He works his way from the bottom up to her clitoris, carefully licking and sucking every part of her pussy. Kelly could feel his hot tongue on her pussy, and her heart was racing as the sensations feel overwhelming. Her body clinched and turns, as he manipulates her every action with the suction of his tongue. He tried to hold her down while he licked and licked her pussy. She was like a beast now, and he had transferred his desires to her, and she now wanted to pleasure him. She could hardly control herself, her moaned were loud and she could feel an orgasm about to come. She looked at him as he used his second most powerful weapon on her.

"Oh Ben," she said in a yearning voice. "Oh, Ben," she said again. This time with more desire, as he increased his momentum, each stroke with his tongue now caused small spasms that ran through her body.

"Oh God, Ben," she moaned as her fingers dig into the sheets. "God, shit, am gonna cum," she said. Her body twisted and turned; he held tightly onto her pelvis area, she opens her eyes, and he pushed his tongue deep down inside her pussy.

Licking it viciously now, he could see that she was about to go wild, she could not remain still. He gripped her clitoris with his tongue and nibbles on it, and looks up at her and said,

"Don't move, Kelly, you want to talk shit, right? You're so bad right, don't move," he said as he punishes her with his tongue. She was now at his mercy, and was enjoying every minute of it.

"Oh baby, "she moaned, "Please, don't stop."

"I won't," he said as he continued licking and sucking her hot wet pussy. Kelly closed her eyes tightly as she tried to reach for the sweet ecstasy feeling that was running down her body.

"Oh god, shit, Oh, Oh, Shit, Uh, uhhhhhhhhh!" she moaned as she reaches this sweet ecstasy. Her pussy was dripping with her cum. Kelly tried to take a few minutes to calm down, but before she could, Ben was back on the attack; this time with his most powerful weapon, his big black dick. She did not even see it coming because her eyes were closed but her legs were wide open; he slammed his dick inside her pussy as hard as he could. She almost sprung off the bed at the impact. He had a huge dick, it was a monstrous cock. Her eyes popped open and she looked up and realized that he had already mounted her and he was now riding her pussy, with a wicked look in his eyes. She could tell that tonight would be one that she really enjoyed.

As he thrust his dick inside her, he began speaking to her with every thrust, harder and deeper than the last.

"You think you could talk shit, don't you?" he said and gave her a hard thrust.

"Oh," she shrieked.

"Don't you?" he said, this time even harder.

"Noooo," she moaned.

"Yeah you do," he said with another hard

thrust.

"No, no," she said, as she tried to escape his deep hard thrust by trying to hold onto his pelvis to reduce the force of each penetration.

"Yeah, you havei a big mouth," he continued, but this time, he started slamming his dick inside her violently. The bed shook and shook, and it seemed like it would have broken; the sound of his skin against hers with every slam was like a whiplash on her skin. She cried and moaned for almost an hour. He was torturing her, but he was also torturing himself because he was trying very hard to hold back, he didn't know how much more he could take before exploding inside her pussy.

He grabbed her by her neck and fucked her hard, up, up, and up, his dick went inside her. It got to the point where she was really enjoying being punished with his dick, and he realized that when her painful moaned turned to pleasurable "oozes and ahhsss," he couldn't believe it, here he was fucking her and trying to teach her a lesson, and she was enjoying every rough hard stroke.

Before he could turn her around and fuck her in her ass, he felt his hot liquid exploding out of his dick.

"God Damn!" he groaned, his dick throbbing inside her, while his hot cum was dripping out along the back of her pussy. He looked down at her, and he stopped for a minute and he could feel the tiny contractions inside her; he knew she had just had another orgasm. She also had a glow on face, as she smiled at him. He tried to remain angry but he could not, he really loved this woman, and every time he tried to pull back away from her, she would just pull him right back. She was mean and evil, but even worse, she was a temptress. He lay down beside her and fell asleep.

When Ben woke up the following morning he realized that he was dealing with 'cool Kelly.' She was sweet to him, and had made him breakfast in bed. He sat up and enjoyed the pancakes with some chocolate syrup.

"What do you have going in today baby?" she asked him.

"Work," he said laughing, "what do you have going on, missy?" he replied to her. He had been busy with work almost every day. His company was working with one of their major clients, and he being the chief engineer, was required to be at work six days a week. She, on the other hand, was a freelance writer, and spent her days writing, and her nights, clubbing. "Well I was thinking that after work we could probably go to the movies or something; do something fun to get out of the house," she said. He thought about it for a while and thought that might be a good idea if he was able to got out of the office early. During recent times he had been doing some late nights at the office, but it was all in an effort to complete this new project so that he could take her on a surprise vacation to the

Bahamas.

"Yeah, sure, why not?" he replied. Ben enjoyed his breakfast and got up to get ready for work. When he was done, he took his shower, got dressed and left for work. He gave her a kiss when he left, hoping that her mood would not change by the time he got home.

The drive to work was horrible. There was so much traffic, and Ben thought that he would never make it to the office. He walked in about twenty minutes late; he could hardly believe how his morning had changed from good to bad. As he looked into his office he could see the figure of a man standing there.

He didn't know who it was but he knew it was not a good sign because the only people who had access to his office were the president and the director of the company. He opened the door, and to his dismay, Mr. Cooper, the Director was in his office.

"Good morning Paul, I'm so sorry you had to be waiting for me like this, please have a seat. Traffic was horrible this morning, I'm so sorry," he apologized profusely to his boss.

"Oh that's not a problem Ben," Mr. Cooper replied. Ben sighed with relief when he heard these words and his tone of voice. "You can relax Ben, I actually had some good news for you," he said laughing. "We had to let one of our top Senior Chief Engineers in Miami go, so now, we looking to replace him, and we think that you are just the person we need to go down there," he continued.

"Oh wow," Ben said in shock, he really did not expect this at all.

"It's actually a promotion, we would provide

an apartment, a car, and a ten percent raise for you," he continued.

"Wow," Ben was so shocked he could hardly reply.

"We would need you to go there by the weekend, and it might be a permanent position so we would understand if you may not want to do it, but personally, I think you should take this opportunity." he said looking at Ben as if waiting for an answer.

"Well, umm, it sounds like a great opportunity, Mr. Cooper. Don't got me wrong, but, I don't know if it's too sudden. Can I think about it today, since its Monday and I would got back to you by Thursday at the latest," Ben replied.

"Yeah sure, but don't forget, Ben, once in a lifetime opportunity." Mr. Cooper said as he ended their conversation and headed out the door.

Ben could not believe his luck, he knew he had a short space of time to make his decision, but deep down inside he really wanted to move away from Ruston. He had grown up in this small town, and he felt that now would be a great time to pack up and leave for a bigger city.

He could hardly wait to tell Kelly, he picked up the phone and dialled her number to share the good news with her. When she answered the call she was in a great mood, but her mood took a drastic turn when she heard the news, what should had been good news seemed like he had just informed her that the world was about to end. She screamed and shouted at him, telling him that he was inconsiderate and not thinking about her in this situation. The bottom line was that she was not about to pack her bags and head down to Miami in a week to follow him and his dreams.

"What about what am doing over here" she shouted.

"What are you doing Kelly, you are going to miss your stupid, whoosh friends to party with? Is that it?" he shouted back at her. In the end she hung up, and he felt like she just did not support anything that he wanted.

That night when Ben got home, he and Kelly had their most vicious fight ever. Bottles were thrown across the room and although it did not get physical, the fight was very emotionally heated. All sorts of bad suppressed memories were brought up, in the exchange of words."You killed our baby!" he shouted at her. "You and your wild partying. If you had been at home resting like every other pregnant woman I know, we would have beautiful baby right now,"he continued.

"How could you," she shouted back at him. "How could you blame me for that, I loved that baby more than you, Ben, I was the one carrying her inside me, you big jerk!" she shouted at him, with her eyes filled with tears. This was it for Ben; he was done with this woman. He was done with all the drama, the rumors and everything. He had loved her and tried to give her everything that she wanted but all he got in return was hatred, unkind words, and unfaithfulness.

Yes he knew about her cheating lying ways. It was the talk of the town, and when she would come home with love bites on her neck, or a new necklace or earrings. She always had an excuse, but he had put up with all the bad things because he loved her. However, now when he needed her to be supportive and he thought that she would actually appreciate the move and change of environment, here she was, treating him like he had just told her he killed her mom.

The week went by quickly and soon Ben was on his flight to Miami, Kelly did not even come to drop him off at the airport, she was at the apartment when he left. He had told her that he would continue to pay the rent, until he could move all his stuff out of the apartment, had left his car with his best friend Robert.

Miami was quite a change from Ruston; first, it was a more vibrant, lively city. There were big hotel buildings everywhere, and the people there were mostly blacks, and Hispanics. He had a beautiful condo, on the fifth floor of a luxury apartment complex, and he had been given his own personal assistant named Nia. This was everything he had ever dreamed of; he did, however, regret that he was not able to share this time of his life with the woman that he had loved so dearly.

As he sat in his new office, he looked around and enjoyed the moment, his assistant came to mind. Nia was a slender young woman of Puerto Rican descent; you could tell from the way that she rolled her tongue when she spoke. Her hair was light brown, almost blonde, and she had a beautiful, soft, tanned complexion. If he weren't so consumed with his thoughts of Kelly, he would have pursued his new attractive personal assistant. He now understood, why so many of his friends fell for their personal assistants.

As time went by, Ben slowly started to adjust to his new job, and his new home, it had now been about five months since he left Ruston, and Kelly Wild-fire, behind. As he got ready to leave the office, Nia, came to drop off the technical report on his desk. She was wearing a tight black pencil skirt with a pink blouse. He sat at his desk and as she bent over to put the report on his desk he saw her cleavage. She had her hair tucked back in a ponytail and she wore light pink lipstick. When he saw the slight peak of her breast, he was aroused.

He had not been with any woman in months; he had been too consumed with work and his former girlfriend to even think about sex. However, now the feelings were coming back to him, and he wanted his personal assistant. At that moment he wanted to fuck her right there in his office. He looked up and he could see the look in Nia's eyes, he could tell that she wanted him. He swallowed hard, as she walked over to the back of the desk where he was sitting.

"I see you looking at me Ben, all the time," she told him in a seductive voice. "I know you want me," she continued as she proceeded to sit down on his lap.

He did not resist her; he instantly began kissing her hard. Her lips were soft and tender and as they kissed she begun stripping off her clothes, and then his clothes. She then began gliding her tongue gently along the nape of his neck. Ben groaned as he enjoys the sensations he's been missing out on.

Their bodies were hot with desire, and soon he put her naked body on his desk. She pulled down her panties which were all she had left on. Her pussy was beautiful, with small brown hairs running along the center of it. He began to gently stroke her pussy with her fingers, she moaned with pleasure, and the look in her eyes lets him know, that she wanted more. He was so horny he could feel his dick about to explode; he quickly whipped it out of his pants, and gently penetrated her pussy.

He realized that she's shocked to see the size of his big dick, she moaned out loud with the first thrust. Her breasts were shaped like small melons and he gently caressed them with his fingers as he had his way with her on the desk.

"Aye papi," she moaned in her native language, and he's turned on even more. He increases his momentum and he could see her breasts bouncing up and down as he continued to thrust his big dick inside her pussy. "Ayyee, papi, si, oh yeah!" she moaned.

He enjoys fucking her wet pussy, and when he felt like he was about to explode, he pulled his dick out of her tiny pussy, and his cum shoots out all over her stomach. His cum was hot and whitish. He looks at her, and she looks fulfilled. They were both exhausted and relaxed for a minute before tidying up and leaving the office.

"You're about eighteen weeks along, Kelly," Dr. Greyson confirms. Kelly had noticed that she was putting on weight, especially in her stomach area, and her menstrual cycle, although irregular, had stopped completely for about four months now. She did feel a little nauseous a couple of mornings but didn't think anything of it.

"How could I not know this," she thought to herself. She had been sure that all the weight she was putting on was due to the fact that she was depressed and going through a painful breakup, but now finding out she was pregnant, clarified a few things. She knew that it was Ben's baby; it had been over a year since she last cheated on him, so it was physically impossible to be impregnated by someone else.

This pregnancy was a hard pill to swallow, considering the fact that she had not seen Ben in over four months, and they hardly spoke on the phone. How would she break the news to him, he probably hated her, how would he ever accept her and this baby? Kelly walked out of the doctor's office, sadder than she had ever been in her life. Even more so she was scared: what if this baby died just like the baby she had been carrying two years ago.

When she got home Kelly called her mom, Marlin and shared the news with her.

"You gotta let that man know, baby," she told her. Kelly always enjoyed talking to her mom because she always ended up feeling better at the end of their conversation. However, this time she felt even worse than before, the thought of having to call Ben to tell him that she was pregnant made her feel nauseous.

Kelly ran to the bathroom and threw up all over the toilet. She called Ben's office immediately, and told him that she would be in Miami that weekend, and they needed to talk. She was surprised he sounded anxious to see her.

Ben was elated to hear from Kelly, and finding out that she would be in Miami was the best thing ever. He was so sorry that he had gotten so upset and left her without trying to make their relationship work. He really wanted to see her to apologize for his behavior and to find out how life was going for her.

Soon it was the weekend, and he sat there at the table at La Palif, Café, waiting for her. It was about two in the afternoon. He saw someone who looked like her in the distance, but this person was bigger than Kelly, had she put on some extra weight. As she came closer his jaw dropped in shock, she was, she was PREGNANT, he thought to himself.

"Kelly, what's going on?" Ben said in an angry voice. He could not believe this, it had just been around five months and she was already pregnant by another man. "How could you, it's not even been five months, whose baby was this?" he demanded. As she sat down, she could not believe he would think so lowly of her,

"This is your baby of course, I've not been with anybody else," she replied. He did not believe her and he told her to her face. "I swear on my momma's life, this is your baby, I've not been with anybody but you. I promise you that, I thought I was just putting on weight, I just found out this week," she explained.

Upon hearing Kelly swearing on her mom's life, he felt deep down inside that she was being honest. He broke down; right there at the café, he could not believe that he had turned into that guy, the guy that walked out on his pregnant girlfriend. He asked her to come back to his apartment so that they could talk some more about this.

When they got to the condo, he apologized over and over. His eyes were filled with tears and his heart was filled with remorse. Kelly knew that he was truly sorry; she, too, had changed from her wild partying days. She had genuinely loved Ben, and she secretly hoped that he would take her back knowing that she was carrying his baby.

"That's ok, I'm sorry for hurting you and not being supportive. I regret it every day," she replied.

When he heard that, he knew that this was

a different Kelly. The Kelly he knew would never apologize to anyone. He gently kissed her lips and they were filled with desire, he could tell that she wanted him. In fact they both wanted each other badly, as their bodies move rhythmically to each other's touch.

Ben continued kissing her softly moving his tongue slowly along her neck and down to her big, full breast. Her body looked even more enticing now that she was carrying his seed inside her. He led her into his bedroom and laid her softly on his bed.

He gently caressed her tender breasts; she moaned as her fingers run through his wavy hair. He gently licked and sucked her breasts; his greatest desire was to please her and to show her how sorry he was for walking out on her and their baby. She looks down at him, and licked her lips, "I'm sorry about everything," she told him.

He looked up at her and said, "You don't have to be sorry baby, I'm sorry. I'm sorry for walking out on you, I'm the one who sorry," he replied.

He could see that her eyes were filled with tears and this was really emotional for her. He gently moved his tongue down along her body, from her breast to her belly, kissing it, and talking to his unborn child. "It's gonna be ok, little baby," he said as he gently kissed and rubs her big belly.

Her belly was round, and unlike most pregnant women, she had no stretch marks. He moved his tongue downward, and gently kissed her pussy, he knew that he had to be gentle and although he would love to suck her pussy, he had heard rumors that it could be dangerous for the baby.

Kelly realizes that Ben was shaky as he was extremely gentle with her; she decided to take things into her own hands. She got up and asked him to stand up at the edge of the bed, she sat at the edge of the bed and gently cupped his dick in her hand, and his dick was just as big and long as she remembered.

She slowly placed her tongue on it, and licked it. He tilted his head back and groaned. Kelly then slowly put his entire dick in her mouth and gives it a long hard suck.

Ben almost went crazy. She then began to suck his dick, vigorously, giving it long hard sucked while moaning. Then she orders him to lie down on the bed, and got on top of him. She slowly slides herself down on his huge dick. As he felt her warm pussy sliding down on his dick, Ben moaned,

"Oh Kelly Wild-fire."

She looks at him and puts her finger to his lips and whispers, "Kelly Wildey, baby," insinuating that she's changed and no longer went by that name. He was even more impressed tried hard to keep still as she used her pussy to ride him. It was the sweetest most pleasurable feeling he had ever felt. She went up and down on his dick, her pussy was so wet and hot, and he could not resist his desire to slam his dick inside her. He gently held onto her butt cheeks and gave her a quick slam, she shrieked loudly.

"I'm sorry," he said immediately, afraid that he had hurt her. How ironic, the last time he had fucked her, he was trying to hurt her, but now he just wanted to be gentle with her. As she enjoyed his dick, her full breasts were bouncing up and down. He could see her licking her lips and he could hear her moaning with pleasure.

He realized that his feelings for her never went away and the time they had spent apart only made his desires for her more intense, he now wanted to marry this woman. She continued riding his dick, and when she felt like she was about to orgasm, her movements were faster and harder, and she tilted her head back and gave a loud,

"OOOOOOOOOOOOOOOO, BABY," she moaned. He too was about to explode inside her, he looked deep into her eyes, as their movements and their bodies became one, as they reached their climax and exploded with ecstasy. He could swear that the neighbors heard them when they were coming.

"O God, I love you so much Kelly," he said.

"I love you too, Benjamin Davis," she replied. They held each other for the rest of the afternoon into the night.

Kelly and Ben now live in Miami with their baby Carina. They were married three months after Kelly gave birth and they often spend their time walking in the park with their daughter and having good family time together. Everything turned out great for this couple and Kelly Wild-fire now went by another name Mrs. Kelly Wildey-Davis.

10 HOME INVASION SENSATIONS

It was the night before his trip to Chicago and Lisa wanted to ensure that her husband would miss everything about her.

As she prepared his dinner, her R. Kelly CD was playing in the background. Her breasts were exposed bare, and she covered her white lace thong with a short, red apron. As she heard the keys rattling at the front door, she popped open a bottle of champagne and poured two glasses, one for herself and one for her husband.

After standing in the kitchen waiting for a while, she finally made her way to the living room to greet her husband. She almost fainted when she saw a masked man holding her husband at gunpoint. Instantly the glasses that she was holding in her hands dropped to the floor making a loud crashing sound. Her frantic scream pierced the air as the feelings of panic and fear consumed her.

"Stop screaming or I will shoot him. And then shoot you!" the man shouted angrily. Lisa was in such shock that although she wanted to stop screaming she could not.

The angry man hit her husband hard over his head with his gun, causing him to fall to the floor unconscious. He then launched himself across the living room to grab Lisa.

"You wanna scream, I'll give you something to scream about," he said as he used his huge masculine hand to squeeze her throat, while holding her up against the wall.

He wore a dark black stocking over his face with only two small openings for his eyes. As he braced her firmly against the wall his tongue radically forced its way into her mouth. She was very reluctant and tries to struggle with him. She managed to briefly pull her lips away from his. "Please, don't do this, please," she begged but he was unmoved by her cries, and continued his invasion of her mouth, lips and tongue. As she wiggled her body to try to escape his firm lock, she was forced to stop when he increased the pressure of his massive hand on her throat. Grasping for air, Lisa finally gave in and relaxed a little as he proceeded to explore the rest of her petite body.

The huge man scooped her up in his arm and brought her upstairs opening the first door to his right which led to her bedroom. He laid her on the bed and used a pair of handcuffs he had in his back pocket to cuff her to the headboard.

Then he pulled yet another surprise from his pocket; it was a mouth gag, and some rope. Lisa wiggled her body violently as she tried desperately to escape from him. He held the gun to her head, looked into her hazel eyes and said, "Stop."

He had used a soft yet firm, frightening tone of voice, that had shivers running down Lisa's spine. When he was done tying her down with her legs spread wide as she lay all but naked in the bed, he put on the finishing touches by using the mouth gag to block off her screams.

He placed the gun near the temple of her head, and whispered "Don't move," then swiftly made his way out of the room. Minutes later he returned with Thomas, at gun point. "Now, I want you to suck her pussy like you've never done before," he instructed.

Clearly Thomas was frightened, because he immediately got down between her legs and begun flicking his tongue against her tender, bare flesh. Lisa's eyes popped open and at that moment she completely forgot that there was another man in the room with them. Thomas moved his tongue slowly up and down the small opening of her vagina, and then with a strong suction grip he took hold of her clit with his mouth. Lisa's head spun, as her juices begun trickling down her body. Her toes curled and her fingers gripped the sheets as the intensity of the sensations engulfed her body.

"Lick that clit... harder," the man instructed as he moved closer point the gun at Thomas.

He did as he was told and the stroke of his tongue on her clitoris became more vulgar, and he ate her pussy like he was hungry for it.

He devoured every inch of her hot wet cunt, and she yearned to have her insides penetrated with his dick. Thomas too, was now getting weird sensations running through his body; his cock throbbed with desire in his pants.

"Nigga, suck that bitch. I wanna see her lose control. I wanna see it in her eyes, c'mon now, gimme more!" the man shouted angrily as he continued to point the gun at her husband. After hearing these instructions, Thomas gave in and he let his desire to control his every moment. He plunged his hot tongue deep down inside her pussy, and sucked hard, then pulled it out, only to penetrate the hole again with his tongue. This time when he pulled out his tongue he could see her knees shaking wildly and he could tell that she was on the brink of her climax. Without any word from the stranger, he plunged his tongue deep inside her again. But this time, he licked and sucked the entire pussy like she had never done before.

Her pussy contracted as tiny spasms ran through her cunt. Lisa closed her eyes, and gyrated her groin area, against his mouth. He used his tongue to drive her wild and finally she reached her climax. Her eyes closed tightly, as she gripped the sheets and her toes curled as she exploded in his mouth. Thomas released the grip he had on her with his tongue and her slightly elevated pussy fell down unto the bed, as it her juices trickled down her inner thighs.

"Good. Very Good. Now she's ready to suck my dick," the invader said with a wicked smile on his face.

"CUT!" Thomas said as he got off his wife and walked over to the man who had now put away the gun he had been holding.

"You're doing great honey!" he said to his wife, giving her a thumbs up as he and the other guy chatted a bit.

Lisa Spearman was a petite woman with a tanned complexion; she was of Afro-Asian descent. She had been married to her husband Thomas Spearman for about one year, and they were constantly trying new adventurous things to spice up their relationship. Her job as a full-time nurse kept her away from home most of the time but when she did get to be at home, she made up for all their time apart. Thomas worked as a college football coach and spent his time on the road with his team.

However this was the first time that they would be filming their role playing. This was also the first time that they would enjoy the company of an outside party during one of their intimate encounters.

The guy holding the gun, and playing the role of the intruder, was her husband's best friend Jerry. Thomas and Jerry had met in college and had developed a close bond and they were like brothers. Therefore when the subject of having a 'ménage-a-trios' came up, they decided to ask Jerry if he wanted to participate. Lisa was happy to use Jerry instead of one of her female friends, because although she trusted herself, she did not trust other females around her husband. Too many couples had met the end after a somewhat harmless threesome with a close girlfriend.

As she lay in the bed she could see her husband and Jerry reviewing the recording on the camcorder. While the two men chatted, her imagination got the best of her, as she envisioned what it would be like to be with two men at the same time. Two dicks penetrating your pussy at the same time, or one dick in the pussy and another in the ass.

Suddenly her arousal peaked and she motioned her husband to release her from her cuffs and other restrictions. They had previously planned the event, and it was agreed that there would be no genital penetration on Jerry's end. However her wandering mind was now causing her to have a change of heart. Would her husband agree to let his friend fuck her? Was the question that lingered in her mind?

The two men smiled at her when she got to where they had been standing. "You enjoying it baby?" Thomas asked his wife. "Yep, it's going great," she replied as she tried to find a tactical way to suggest that she wanted to have both men fuck her.

"Umm, I was just thinking. What if we switch things up a bit, you know, took it up a notch," she said with a smile on her face.

"Yeah, sure," her husband answered, as he waited to hear her suggestions. "Well, I was kinda interested in doing, like... you know," she stopped and took a deep breath as the two men looked at her with curious eyes, waiting to hear her request.

"Well like, you know, a double penetration or something, you know, like in the movies," she finished.

Thomas was shocked to hear something like this coming out of his wife's mouth. He had secretly dreamed about it, but he never even suggested doing it for fear that she might get offended. He looked over at Jerry, who had nearly popped out when he heard her suggestion. Looking back at his wife he asked her if she was sure she wanted to do that. When she confirmed that she did not mind trying it out, he could not hide the excitement and anxiety that he felt. "Well let's do this then," Jerry said as he walked over to the camcorder to set it on record. Everyone got back in the former position and they proceeded to shoot their hot, steamy, Home Invasion porno.

"And action!" Thomas said as he got back between the legs of his naked wife who was once again cuffed to the bed. Jerry stood in the corner with his gun pointed at them. He spread her pussy lips with hand and gave it a few hard strokes.

"Now, I want you to fuck this bitch!" Jerry said from the corner where he was standing. Thomas whipped out his semi-hard dick, and stroked it a couple of times with his hand, to get it to the right degree of hardness. Then he penetrated her tight little pussy with his huge dick. Although Lisa could not scream out, she did moan and a muffled noise could be heard through her mouth gag. Upon hearing her reaction, Thomas began to thrust his dick inside her pussy until it was wet and hungry with desire. He fucked her giving her long hard strokes at first. He pulled his dick in and out her pussy, as her body squirmed under pressure of his massive cock.

"Oh yeah, baby, that's my fucking shit," he said, as thrust his dick in and out her pussy. Lisa managed to give him a little smile and a wink as he fucked her.

"Oh yeah, ooo, yeah, babbyyy..." he grunted as he increased the momentum of his thrusts.

Lisa's pussy was warm and inviting and as his dick explored her insides, she could feel her juices pouring out like a fountain. She was in sweet ecstasy and she closed her eyes as she allowed him to take full control of her pussy.

At his hardest, Thomas definitely had one of the largest dicks in the world. It was dark brown, with big, bulging veins running across it, with a purplish pink round head. As he penetrated her insides she could feel his dick hitting hard against her pussy walls. Although painful at first she soon got into the rhythm and was really enjoying her husband's huge cock.

Thomas groaned out loud as he felt her pussy contracting against his dick, and her wet cunt almost had him going crazy.

Meanwhile Jerry stood in the corner with glutinous eyes, as he too, was getting an immense arousal. He unzipped his pants and made a loud "aww," when he whipped out his hard dick.

In the heat of the moment Lisa had forgotten that they were not alone, her eyes opened when she heard loud groaned coming from the corner of the room. It was then that her eyes caught a glimpse of Jerry's long, hard dick. She could barely see much of it, but from the little that she could see, she was impressed with its length.

"No wonder, he had been quite the player. He was packing long and hard," she thought to herself as she closed her eyes again to focus her attention on her impending climax.

Their bodies jerked back and forth together, and she could see the sweat trickling down the sides of Thomas's forehead. "Oh shit, baby, I'm gonna cummmmmmmmmmm!" he groaned as he gave her the longest, hardest stroke in the series.

She pushed her body upwards as she met his downward thrust halfway. They both exploded and climaxed together. As their bodies fell to the bed, they could hear Jerry still groaning in the background.

"Damn, that was a good show," he said with his hard long dick in his hand. "I think we need to cut for a bit," he continued and walked over to the camcorder.

The three of them took a break and all came together as they reviewed the taped scenes of their homemade pornographic video. They did not want to admit it they were all quite anxious to get back and film their last scene together: their ménage-a-trios scene. As they were speaking Lisa could not stop fantasizing about Jerry. He had been quite the ladies' man, and several women that he had been with had almost gone crazy when he broke up with them. Could this be the reason why, could it be because of his long dick. She had never in past fantasized about another man, in the presence of her husband, but here she was with him fantasizing about fucking his best friend.

As she stood there, her thoughts were interrupted by the voice of her husband. "What?" she asked since she had not heard his question. He looked at her with a curious expression; he could tell that something was on her mind, and he feared that it might be her having second thoughts about their threesome. "I said, do you want us to do double penetration, in your pussy, or do you want each of us to fuck one of your holes?" he asked her again.

"Well, I could try both and we could switch it up, baby," she said with a slight smile on her face. Jerry, who had been silent almost the entire time, finally spoke and mentioned something about he wanted to use a vibrator he had brought.

They all laughed hard. "You were ready, weren't you," Thomas said to him laughing.

"I think we should have a drink before we got to this scene y'all," Lisa said as she made her way to the small bar on the side of the kitchen and poured each of them a shot of Bacardi. While close to the kitchen she realized that it had been about two hours and the turkey she had in the oven was about ready. "I also have dinner ready you guys!" she shouted at the top of her lungs so the men who were in the living room area could hear.

They were all walking around in the house buck naked, and the two men were horny at the sight of Lisa parading her naked flesh around them. As she brought them their drinks, Thomas could not resist the urge to smack her perfectly shaped bottom. A loud smack as she jolted forward when she felt the impact of his hard, masculine hand on her bare skin. Jerry laughed loud, when he saw her reaction to her husband's smack. "I'd love to have a go at that," he said winking at Thomas. "I mean, sure, go ahead, you had a pass for today," Thomas replied laughing.

He did not have to tell Jerry twice. Jerry lipped at the open invitation and smacked Lisa two times on her butt really hard. Lisa looked at him, with intense eyes as if telling him, she did not approve of his behavior.

"C'mon Lisa, Thomas said I could," Jerry said, when he saw the anger flash in her eyes. As they sat around sipping on their drinks Lisa realized that the men both had erect dicks, and she herself was aroused.

Lisa sprung from her seat and walked over

to where her husband was seated. "So," she said, "about the ménage-a-trios... I think I want it right here, right now," she continued as she gave him a devious look. Thomas' eyes lit up but it was Jerry who got the most excited. His dick stood at attention as he watched Lisa passionately kiss her husband.

"Can I join now?" he asked in an anxious voice. Lisa turned her attention to Jerry and replied, "Yeah, baby it's a three-some, ain't it?" winking with one eye.

Jerry jumped up from his seat and headed straight to the horny couple with his hard dick in his hand. When he got to them he immediately began stroking her nipples with his thumb and forefinger. She moaned out from the pleasure as he worked his fingers on her tits.

Thomas stood up and held her up in his arms, and made his way to the center of the room. He lay across the floor with his erect dick upwards. He pulled Lisa over him and slid his erect cock into her pussy. Jerry swiftly made his way over to her with a small bottle of lube. He used his fingers to spread the lube around and inside her anus. Then without warning he found a comfortable position behind her, and while Thomas had his dick in her pussy he thrust his long dick upwards into her ass.

"Oh shit!" Lisa shrieked as she felt the sudden pain from the penetration of his long dick into her ass. Jerry gripped her ass cheeks and continued to force his way upwards inside her. This was nothing like she had ever felt before. Lisa had not known how this would feel but now she was not sure how much more of this double penetration she could handle. The muscles inside her anus fought hard to prevent this intrusion of Jerry's long dick. He gripped her flesh and thrust his dick hard into her ass, causing her to spring upwards, in an effort to escape his huge tool.

Meanwhile her husband, Thomas, was comfortably ramming his dick inside her hot wet pussy. He gave her several long hard thrusts with his huge dick, which caused her to cry out his name.

"Oh, Thomas!" she moaned as she tried hard to bear the pain and sensations that she felt. Somehow Thomas and Jerry had managed to get their thrusts in synchronized rhythms. As they pounded her pussy and ass, Lisa cried out with mixed feelings.

She felt like her holes were being torn apart by these two disastrous cocks. As they continued slamming their dicks inside her all the pain that she had been feeling gradually began to subside as a feeling of immense pleasure took over.

"Yes, yes," she shouted in her ecstasy. This must be what people in the pornos feel, she thought to herself, as she embraced the entirely new sensations that she was now feeling. The men were both moaning and groaning as their dicks controlled their every movement.

"Oh God Lisa, Lisa," Thomas groaned as he penetrated her deeper and deeper. His dick was now rocking her insides. The pressure of the two men working their dicks in her pussy and ass sent violent shock waves through her.

She tried hard to ride her husband's dick but the impending pressure of Jerry's dick in her ass made it almost impossible. Finally she just let go and allowed the two men to take control of her exhausted body.

Some of the strokes were long and hard, while others were fast and hard. They were all covered with sweat, and their sounds of their moans filled the air like they were doing a musical together. Lisa looked down into Thomas eyes, and she could see that he was definitely enjoying this. She leaned downwards and when her lips met his they devoured each other's tongues. They were both very passionate about each other and Jerry could tell. At that moment he felt a little sense of jealousy.

He longed to have a beautiful wife, like Lisa, who would do anything to please him and make him happy. As these jealous thoughts lingered in his mind, he decided to give her a little taste of what she was missing. As she had leaned over to kiss her husband, this position allowed Jerry greater access inside her ass. With all his force, he shoved his dick hard inside her, causing her to jerk forward.

Both Lisa and Thomas felt the impact of his thrust and the pleasure that they had been feeling increased. Jerry continued to pound the insides of her ass with his long dick causing her lips to break away from her husband's, as she moaned out loud. "Oh God, Oh God," she moaned as she closed her eyes.

Thomas looked up at Jerry and caught a glimpse of the wicked little smile that he had in the corner of his lips. He was furious that his friend would pull a stunt like this. So, this was a competition, he thought to himself. With that thought, he engulfed her lips with his mouth, to bring her attention back to him, then begun his attack on her pussy. He thrust his dick as hard as he could upwards inside her. She shrieked in pain and pleasure, and her tongue gripped him tighter, as she felt him increase the force of his thrusts inside her pussy.

As she was sandwiched between the two men Lisa, could feel her holes expanding to accommodate their vicious attacks. Her body moved in rhythm with theirs and as they increased the momentum of their strokes, her juices gushed down the core of her womanhood. She was like a caged beast, full of life and wanting to release. As they fucked, they all felt the magical sensations and the thrusts of men increased as their dicks explore her insides.

"Holy shit, I'm cumming! Oh shit, oh shittttttttt!" Thomas groaned out loud as he exploded inside her pussy. At the same time, Jerry grabbed her long curly hair as slammed his dick hard inside her asshole, and pulled it out, spraying his hot cum all over her ass. Lisa herself moaned out as she herself reached her sensational climax. Her pussy contracted as she squirted out her juices on Thomas' dick.

The three of them, got up and sat on the couch naked and exhausted. Her pussy and her asshole were sore from all the pounding. Lisa realized that in their haste they had forgotten to switch on the camcorder in the living room area. So basically they had nothing on camera for their "ménage-a-trios" scene.

"Oh darn it, we forgot to switch on the camera," she said, as she looked at her husband, was just as exhausted as she was. He barely opened his closed eyes and replied, "Just give me a minute; we'll get back to it."

Lisa could feel the pain of all the penetration that she had been getting, and she knew even if she wanted more, her body would not be able to handle any more. She looked over at Jerry, who also had his head leaned back against the wall, and she knew he probably was very tired also. She carefully examined his naked body with her eyes. He had a lean, handsome body; his chocolate brown skin glistened with the sweat droplets that were on it. For a minute she wished that she would feel his dick inside her pussy instead of inside her ass. Oh God, what a wicked thought, she thought to herself, as she closed her eyes, biting on her lower lip, imaging how it would feel to had Jerry's long dick thrusting inside her pussy.

They sat on the couch for a while then got dressed and went to the kitchen to enjoy a delicious turkey dinner. After dinner, Jerry made his way home, while Lisa and her husband got ready for bed. As they lay down in the bed, Thomas cuddled her in his arms as he caressed her tender nipples with two of his fingers. Lisa could feel herself getting horny all over again, but her swollen pussy and paining asshole made her resist his touch.

"Can we continue this tomorrow?" she asked as she planted a soft gentle kiss on his lips and turned with her back facing him. She was soon fast asleep.

The following morning when they woke up, life went on as usual. Thomas went off to work, while Lisa stayed around the house cleaning and preparing for her evening shift.

The entire day, all that she could think about was their little homemade porno. She also could not rid her mind of her desire to be with Jerry one more time. She felt like a child who had taken to the amusement park, but was only allowed to go on one of the rides. This sucked; she thought to herself, as she plugged her vacuum into the outlet on the wall and proceeded to pass it back on forth on the carpet.

As she got to the center of the living room, she saw the white spots on the red carpet. These spots were the residue left from the ejaculation of semen all over her and inside her. She licked her lips as she sat on the couch. As she sat there, she remembered how exhausted they were after their ménage-a-trios.

It was supposed to be a fun home invasion homemade video, but now, it had turned into much more than that. She was sure that Thomas could tell that she wanted to fuck Jerry again. Even this morning when he kissed her on his way out she had imagined that it were Jerry's lips touching hers. Maybe she had gotten a little taste of his dark chocolate and wanted more, she thought to herself. The more she thought about everything that had happened, the more she wanted to fuck Jerry. Soon she found herself getting wet, and her pussy aching to feel of Jerry's long dick.

She had to do something about it. She went to her computer desk and opened the first drawer, searched way in the back and pulled out a DVD.

'Three's Good Company' was written across the DVD. She popped it into her computer, and sat there with her legs opened, ready to pleasure herself. As the video began playing she watched closely with the erotic sensations building up inside her as she watched the woman in the video got her pussy destroyed by two large cocks at the same time.

Damn, that shit must hurt like a mother... she thought to herself. Her fingers had now made their way under her short skirt into her panties. She soon realized that her pussy was still swollen from last night when she felt the pain as she rubbed her aroused clitoris. She moaned out loud, and went a little gentler with her strokes.

Suddenly there was a hard knock at the door; she leaped from her seat, quickly turning off her computer. She fixed her skirt and calmed herself down as she made her way to the door. Her mouth almost dropped to the floor when she opened her front door.

"Hi, Lisa, could I could come in? I had a confession to make," Jerry said with a smile on his face. She did not know whether she wanted to let him in for fear that she might go behind her husband's back and fulfill her secret desires with him. But her pussy was still throbbing from the video that she had started watching and she needed to climax. She needed to climax, with Jerry's dick in her wet pussy. She slowly let him in, as they gave each other wicked smiles.

Meanwhile, while Thomas was at work, he couldn't help but remember the suspicious looks that he felt his wife giving to his best friend. Although he was one hundred percent sure that she had never cheated on him in the past, this new situation bothered him.

He knew Jerry, and when he wanted a woman, he did not care about anything else; he would go out of his way to get that woman. Had he made a mistake letting Jerry see his wife naked and moreover letting Jerry fuck his wife? He hoped that no matter what that both Jerry and his wife would remain loyal to him and not had sex with each other behind his back.

He loved his wife the thought of her having sex with another man behind his back almost drove him crazy. Her sweet wet pussy, in fact his pussy, because he owned her and she owned his dick, was meant only for him. That's why, although he wanted to experience what it would feel like to see his wife in extreme pain and pleasure from the penetration of two cocks, he did not want anybody else's dick fucking her pussy. Jerry could fuck her in the ass if he was around with his permission, but her pussy was his.

This was where he would put his face, his tongue, his mouth and his dick, and he wanted it all to himself.

The more he thought about everything, the more anxious he became and he decided to call his wife. He pulled his cell phone out of his pocket and dialed their home number. The phone rang and rang, but no one came to answer.

This could not be, when he had left this morning she had said she would do some cleaning up and then go to work; she did not mention that she would be leaving the house. He hit redial and waited patiently for her to answer the phone. Again there was no answer. He called a third and a fourth time and yet there was no answer. What the hell was going on? Before panicking and letting his crazy thoughts got the best of him, he decided to call her on her cell phone. It went straight to voice mail.

At that moment he had enough. He sprung up from his seat and quickly exited the building. As he drove home, all sorts of twisted thoughts clouded his mind. If he found the two of them in bed together, he would not use the fake gun they had while shooting the video. He would use a real gun, he thought angrily to himself.

As he sped through the traffic, his heart raced, as he feared he might catch his wife and his best friend having sex with each other behind his back. He parked his car at a distance about a block away from his house, and walked to his home. As he entered the door his jaw dropped as he saw his wife naked on the couch.

Her fingers were between her legs and she was engrossed in pleasuring herself while watching a porno on her laptop.

"Lisa, what were you doing?" he asked curiously.

"Well Jerry stopped by with his fine self," she laughed. Thomas's heart nearly skipped a beat when he heard that Jerry had indeed stopped by, just like he thought he would.

"And, what did he say?" Thomas asked.

"Well he said, he isn't comfortable doing that kinda stuff, and he was not interested in filming the ménage-a-trios scene," she said.

"So I popped this video in, and started watching people who were comfortable doing that kinda stuff." she said, laughing again.

Thomas breathed a sigh of relief and came to join his wife on the couch. "Now you know you got me right here, you don't need to be watching this, when we could be doing it ourselves," he said as he grinned at her and kissed her lips softly. Lisa went wild when he touched her she was already so wet, this was like adding fuel to her burning desire. He picked her up and brought her upstairs where, he used his tongue, fingers and his huge dick to fuck her. This was definitely better than any ménage-a-trios.

AUTHOR'S NOTE

Readers: I want to expand a few of the stories to see where the characters can be explored further. If there are any of the stories that you would like to read more about again, I'd love to hear from you!

Visit my blog at www.shalabreece.com

Join my newsletter for free exclusive previews
www.shalabreece.com/in

Follow me on Twitter at
www.twitter.com/shalabreece

Like my page on Facebook at
www.facebook.com/shalabreece

Discover my books at major ebook retailers everywhere.